The Burlwood Forest Trilogy

BURLWOOD FOREST

○

THROUGH THE WOODS

○

MANY FIELDS

The Burlwood Forest Trilogy

BURLWOOD FOREST

Written and Illustrated by

JOHN CHOQUETTE

· pumpernickel art

Printed in the United States of America
First Printing, 2014
ISBN 978-0-692-27703-4

Pumpernickel Art
Raleigh, NC
www.burlwoodforest.com
@burlwoodforest

For my amazing wife, Anna. You are awesome.

Grandma Jo,
  You are the BEST!
Thank you <u>so much</u> for
reading Burlwood Forest. I
really appreciate your support!
  THANK YOU!!!!!

John Choquette

Tugley

You might not know it, but Michael Pumpernickel saved the world. Without him, well, it's too hard to even think about where we'd be. So it's no wonder he's so popular! These days, everybody loves him. Parents. Teachers. Doctors. Women. Even his classmates. But it hasn't always been this way. Why, just a few years ago, he was lonely. Desperate. Sometimes, even lonely AND desperate. Not cool at all.

But that was then and this is now. Today, Michael Pumpernickel is a hero! He didn't just become amazing overnight though. It took an event so stunning, an event so important, that it didn't just change his life, it changed the world.

He turned eleven.

I know what you're thinking. Birthdays are fun, but they don't really make a difference, do they? Was he really all that more remarkable at age eleven and zero days than he was at age ten and 364 days? No, not really. In fact, he was just as unremarkable as ever. But you're forgetting something. To Michael Pumpernickel, all the best heroes were eleven. At least they were in the stories he read, and that's really all that mattered.

When you think about a hero, what do you think of? Courage? Strength? Speed? Michael Pumpernickel had none of those things. He was just an ordinary, clumsy kid. Overweight. No friends. You probably wouldn't have wanted to hang out with him either. But turning eleven would change everything, at least in his mind. And as it turns out, he was right.

To get acquainted with our hero, I would like to show you an excerpt from his diary that explains just how excited he was before his eleventh birthday party. He must have known that something big was coming-

Dear, Diary. Mom is planning a HUGE party and all the kids from school are invited. It should be amazing! Miss Dandelion, my piano teacher, is invited too! I've been in love with her as long as I can remember. I really hope everyone comes. I've been working on the invitations since I turned ten. I even made a special collage of all of my favorite things for each person. I just hope they still like

Bingo the Big Blue Dog as much as I do. This is my first real birthday party ever and I want it to be special.

We're going to have pin-the-tail on the donkey, and my dad even hired a clown. The only problem is I don't like clowns. In fact, clowns really scare me! But that's okay. I'll just hide under my bed until he goes away. If I can sneak some cake and ice cream down there it won't be too bad.

Maybe someone will join me? Just not the clown!

Mom said a DJ was too expensive so she hired the organist from our church. Unfortunately, the organ is too big to move so he's bringing a record player (what is that?) and "a lot of great music to jitterbug to." I secretly hope he doesn't come because I don't want to be the only one who doesn't know how to jitterbug. That would ruin my big day.

Well, that or if I spill cake on my birthday outfit. I've got it all picked out. I'm going to wear my favorite green and white striped shirt with the blue collar. I've had it for as long as I can remember. I LOVE that shirt! I think it looks really good with my orange hair. And I like my hair because it looks good with my shirt. It all works out.

The only thing I have left to do for tomorrow is to make the party favor bags. You know, the thing that really

9

seals the deal for the guests. Since I've never had a party though, or even been invited to one, I don't really know what to put in these things. I guess I should probably put money in them, right? I'll ask Mom. She knows everything.

The only time we've disagreed is when she said I couldn't wear my fanny pack to my cousin's wedding. She was totally wrong! I forgave her though because I wore it anyway...UNDER my shirt.

How else was I supposed to carry my entire Hedgemon trading card collection with me? I mean seriously, how else? What if someone there had a Whoopsy and I didn't have the holographic Roongbob they'd want me to trade them? That would have been disastrous! I don't even want to think about it...

You can bet I'll be wearing my fanny pack proudly tomorrow. I just hope I get more Hedgemon cards because then I can wear my BIG fanny pack. It makes me feel dangerous.

(Watch out world!)

So as you can see, Michael was pretty excited about his party. He even reserved two whole chapters in his diary to talk about it. But no one came. Not even his invisible friend Oliver. Here's another excerpt that reveals the depths of his depression following the event-

I was really sad when Oliver didn't show up. We used to do EVERYTHING together! I guess we've grown apart. But if getting stiffed by my best friend wasn't bad enough, I AT LEAST thought my weird brother Ralph would show up. He'd been talking about the party for weeks! Right before cake, he left to go "take Oliver to get a haircut" though. That's ridiculous. Oliver hates Ralph. And Oliver's like 35! Old people are bald!

(Especially, 35-year olds...)

Thankfully, the clown didn't show up either. I can't tell you how happy I was when that happened. Clowns are the worst! Middle-aged men in big shoes and make-up hanging out with children. Does that not sound any alarms for anyone? Sketchy...

The organist was a no-show too, so I hope Mom gets her deposit back. Whatever. Hopefully, he can't come next year either.

I have a confession to make. Technically, someone DID come to my party. Prometheus, our dog, did, even if he didn't want to (and even if he left when he woke up). His name is short for Prometheus the Frightening, Merciless Cat Slayer. Ralph gave him that name. Ralph is SO weird. I really don't get why he's popular, but everybody loves him! Seriously. Ralph got a dog for winning the senior class' 'Most Likely to Succeed Award' as a freshman. Was he even eligible for that? I guess so. He won it every other year too, even as a second-year senior.

Honestly, I had a great time despite the less-than-perfect circumstances. I mean, I don't think my party was all that bad, you know, overall. Nobody came, but that meant I had the cake to myself! Triple chocolate, hot fudge, brownie chunk Oreo, M&M, Reese's cake. Mmmm....It was so good! My stomach still hurts so it must have been great! The best part was probably how moist it was, especially after Prometheus had some. Then it was REALLY moist. I like it moist.

So my party didn't exactly live up to expectations, but next year is going to be way better, I just know it! I wish I could stay up and give you more details, but I can't. Tomorrow is too important.

Think about your favorite thing in the world and then think about that thing's favorite thing in the world and you might begin to understand my excitement. Tomorrow is the first day of school and I'm SUPER excited. School is the chocolate of life. I just LOVE it!

Thank goodness that's over with! Reading Michael's diary is harder than reading the dictionary. He's long winded! But I think you've begun to see the type of person he was as a ten-year old. Pathetic. Friendless. Weird. Really, really weird.

He never actually made it to school the next day which is kind of a bummer for him, but something big happened! Something even better than the first day of school!

Who am I? I'm the Historian! It's my job to document everything that goes on in Burlwood Forest and the surrounding area of Some Town. I know, you've probably never heard of it, but trust me. It's important because that's where the future was saved.

This isn't a short tale. But then again, the greatest tales never are! It's unlike any other you've ever heard. Copyright laws make sure of that. This is the Legend of Burlwood Forest. And it's awesome.

Michael woke up with a start. Today was the day he'd been looking forward to all Summer. It was the end of a three month countdown that began in June when the final school bell rang. You see, while others look forward to the END of school, Michael could hardly wait for it to START.

This is it, he said to himself. *Today is the day that everything changes. My school, my life and maybe even my underwear. Today is the day I make a friend that's real and will actually talk to me. Today is the day I don't take bathroom breaks every five minutes to call Mom. And if I do, then today is the day she actually answers. Today is a big day.*

Today is the first day of sixth grade.

Michael's older brother Ralph had just finished sixth grade a few years ago. Now a junior at the local community college, Ralph was the model of everything Michael wanted to be. Tall, inexplicably handsome and uncontrollably popular. He was the man that everyone talks about when they talk about being 'The Man.' He set every state record in every sport (even the girl's ones) and never had to do his homework because his charm worked on everyone. Even Grumpy Old Ms. Jones.

Ralph is so cool that Michael would have traded his whole Hedgemon collection just to be known as 'Ralph's brother.' Instead, Ralph told everybody he didn't have a brother. Kind of a bummer for Michael.

(No kidding...)

If someone ever saw them together, Ralph would say he was "making our city a better place by helping a poor helpless orphan." Michael thought that whoever the other orphans were, Ralph must be a lot nicer to them.

But things were going to be different. Ralph was supposed to take him to school today in his shiny new sports car to make up for everything he'd ever done. It was all part of a plan established by their Dad to get people to think that Michael was cool. Not that anyone who came after Ralph could be labeled anything but a disappointment.

Ralph was awesome! Michael was...well, we'll be nice. Michael was not, not, not awesome. He didn't think it would work, but if it meant he could spend a longer time saying goodbye to George, he was okay with it.

"Sorry George, I can't bring you today," Michael said with a sad smile. He picked up his teddy bear and gave him a long hug.

Michael and George had been through a lot together. From Aunt Edna's first wedding, to Uncle Arthur's funeral, to Aunt Edna's court appearance and subsequent jailing, George had been there for Michael and it showed. He was a good friend. Michael never let him out of his sight.

What was left of George, and there wasn't much, was Michael's closest companion. He didn't just BELIEVE that George was alive. He knew!

And that makes all the difference you see.

It was at that moment that George's last eye popped off. Perhaps Michael had squeezed him too tightly, but it seemed that the bear was so upset at his friend leaving that he did it himself out of sadness. Either way, it wasn't the ideal situation for anyone. In frustration, Michael threw his bear across the room where it knocked his Distant Galaxy figurine collection into the trash.

"I'm too old for this," he said.

But then he carefully dusted off each piece and rearranged it on his shelf. (I guess he changed his mind). He looked at the smiling faces before him and shuddered when he got to a chrome robot.

I don' t know why, but that guy gives me the creeps. Maybe it's because he reminds me of someone I know? That guy who works at the discount club.

Michael loved Distant Galaxy. He loved it! Ralph didn't. Ralph told him it wasn't cool.

"If HE liked it suddenly it would be," Michael said bitterly. In fact, Ralph HAD gone through a Distant Galaxy phase and it had swept the school like wildfire. It ended when Michael picked it up.

He gazed down at George's limp body and started to cry. George was in the trash can! Once a vibrant symbol of Michael's childhood, the bear had deteriorated with his own hopes and dreams.

(Depressing...)

"Now you can't see me leave so you won't be sad too," he said holding back the tears quite unsuccessfully.

Walking over to the other side of the room, Michael retrieved George's eye. Placing it with care on his dresser, he made a mental note to ask his Mom to sew it back on. He was hoping she wouldn't use it to fix one of his Dad's shirts like last time. Not that the shirt didn't need it. George was kind of creepy with no eyes though.

Looking at his bear, tears ran down Michael's cheeks. *I can't cry like this,* he thought. *I have to be strong for George. After all, Mom says I'm a big boy! I hope she's not just referring to my weight. Man, that would be really mean. I have to stop so I can go to school!*

As he continued to cry anyway, a horrifying thought came to him. It was one of those thoughts you only have when everything you ever believed in is crashing down on you. Maybe that hasn't happened to you yet. But it will.

Or won't if you're lucky.

What if George drowns because I can't stop crying and he gets too wet? Michael thought horrified. *Then I'll REALLY be alone!*

This only made him cry harder and he dove back into his bed, pulling the covers over his head. (A valiant move). Unfortunately, this only made matters worse because he's also horribly afraid of the dark. Figures. On top of that, he could no longer see George so he began to think he might have lost him already. Or worse, that George got up and left!

He's here, Michael told himself. *I just need to be brave. I need to be brave for George.*

(Easier said than done)

Slowly, he gathered himself and lowered the covers. George was sitting right next to him as always. His felt smile was cocked to one side as if to say, "I tricked you best friend." The sight of his bear made Michael smile, a final tear falling from his eyes.

With newfound courage, he got up and walked over to his dresser. It was the first day of sixth grade and he wasn't going to mess around. An occasion like this called for something special.

He reached into the back of the top drawer and pulled out a box. Inside he found exactly what he was looking for. The Fighting Ninja People underwear he got for his birthday last year! (Go ahead, put yours on too). George had given it to him. Well, Ralph had actually boxed up some of Michael's old underwear, unwashed, to play a joke on him, but he didn't know the difference. It was the best gift Michael had ever gotten! He knew that something so great required a monumental occasion and the big day was finally here. Check.

Today HAS to be great, it's school. There's no place I'd rather be, he thought to himself. *Wouldn't it be great if today lasted forever? No,"* he took it back. *"then I couldn't have tomorrow,"* he smiled.

Thinking about school made his heart jump as he raced downstairs expecting to find his whole family waiting to congratulate him on his big day. His Mom had promised him chocolate chip pancakes. Turquoise for the color of his new school. The dolphins.

Instead, he found a completely empty kitchen. Even Prometheus was out somewhere. He never left, he had a cage! Looking around for his pancakes, Michael's eyes landed on an assortment of ingredients at his usual spot at the table. They were all there. Milk, eggs, food coloring and pancake mix.

This might be okay after all, he thought.

Attached to the milk was a note that said, "Make them yourself, I have other stuff to do. Love Mom."

"That WAS nice of her to lay out the ingredients out for me," Michael said. "I can't reach the cabinets. I just wish I knew how to make pancakes."

But being in sixth grade now made him extremely adventurous. He could do anything! He was going to try to make pancakes on his own. (Rebel!) Looking around, he wondered where his Mom kept her cooking supplies.

Thinking back to last night when she made tangled onion sprout soup (which he had only pretended to eat), he remembered that she kept all of her measuring cups in the top cabinet above the refrigerator.

Junk. The old appliance's surface was covered with crayon drawings, arts and crafts and school photos. None of which were his of course.

Ralph sure is good at coloring in the lines, he thought. *And it looks like he had a really great time at the Homecoming dance whenever that was. I wonder why he's with my teacher? She is all red in the face. I wonder if she is embarrassed to be with Ralph?*

His eyes scanned over Ralph's accomplishments. *I wonder why they didn't put any of MY pictures here*, he wondered as he admired a picture of a rhinoceros eating a banana. *And who is Jeff and why in the world do they have HIS pictures?*

Suddenly, something moved below him causing him to jerk into the refrigerator door.

"That kind of hurt," he cursed, looking around for his attacker.

(Okay, that's not much of a curse, but this IS a children's story and cursing is bad to begin with)

He's not up here, Michael thought as he looked towards the ceiling. *And he's not over here,* he decided as he glanced at the walls. *Maybe he's over there!* As Michael took a peek behind the refrigerator, a mouse darted into a hole in the wall. *Aha!* But that wasn't what caught his eye. The BACK of the refrigerator was just as covered with pictures as the front was!

"Hey, those are mine!" he said somewhat satisfied. *Well, at least they're on here.* Gazing fondly at a still life of a bowl of fruit and a fly (what else?), he looked upon the photographic and artistic history of the first eleven years of his life. "I guess Mom wasn't lying when she said she put my pictures on the refrigerator. I just wonder why she put them on the back? I want to know who Jeff is…"

His stomach grumbled. "Oh yeah, pancakes!" he yelled excitedly, scaring even himself. *Whoa.* Shuddering, he jumped when he heard a loud bang in the other room.

"That's funny, no one's home. It couldn't have been the TV....Bingo isn't on yet."

Boy was he puzzled.

Quietly, he tiptoed to the source of the mysterious noise. "If I don't make it through this, Oliver can keep George," he promised. "I don't think they make invisible teddy bears so he probably needs one."

Wanting to get it over with quickly, whatever 'it' was, Michael opened the cabinet beneath the TV covering his face for protection. Instead of whatever he expected, he found Prometheus, curled up in fear, clearly hiding from something, or maybe someone.

"There you are boy! What are you doing? Want to help me make pancakes?" he asked.

Prometheus growled and swung his paw at the door, shutting it in Michael's face.

"That wasn't very nice," he said, hurt by the dog's actions. Looking up at the clock, he quickly realized that it was past time for breakfast. He needed to get to school! *If Ralph's not here, that means I have to go to the bus stop! Drat. I'll just take the ingredients with me and make my pancakes on the way. I don't know if you can do that, but if someone can it's me because I'm in sixth grade.*

(It's sad. Please ask your mom how to cook. Then you'll be prepared if you find yourself in this situation)

Michael quickly gathered the ingredients and put them into his backpack, warm milk and all.

I guess I won't bring any paper today because these eggs sure are taking up a lot of space. Maybe we'll fry eggs on the sidewalk in science class. That would be great. I would eat every single one.

I'm so hungry.

It was one of those mornings where the air is so thick that it feels like you're wearing a full-body sweater. Not the kind you might buy at your favorite store though, whichever one that is. More like the scratchy brown and green plaid sweater your Aunt Edna gives you on your birthday every year. You know, the kind that you return as soon as she goes back home to Cincinnati? THAT one.

Well, it was that kind of day that Michael stepped out into as he carefully shut the front door. After checking the lock three times (who doesn't?), he began his walk to the bus stop, shuffling along the way.

This is the worst, Michael thought. *I may as well just turn around because the bus driver always leaves me when I'm early. Then again...if I'm late?*

About halfway there, he realized he'd left his backpack in his Mom and Dad's room. *How did that even happen? It was on my back?* (Your guess is as good as mine). He'd gone there right before he left to leave them a note saying where he was going. Not that they didn't already know anyway.

Good thing I realized this now, he thought to himself. *There's still five minutes until the bus comes. If I hurry, I might be able to get a seat up front! You know, if he lets me on.*

So Michael turned around and headed back home. As he walked up, he noticed that the flag on the mailbox was down. Wanting to earn responsibility points for his good behavior chart (which in turn, earned him more dessert) he grabbed the mail and began shuffling through it.

I wish email had flags. It's SO much more fun Seriously! he thought. *Wait...This one is to me!!!!!! What?!?!?!*

He was astonished! He'd never gotten mail before. Not on his birthday. Not on holidays. He was already planning on not sending graduation announcements because he figured nobody would read them. Forget Christmas cards...

He turned the letter over, but he couldn't find a return address. *Who is this from?!?* he wondered. Wanting to savor his first-ever piece of mail, he stared at the front of the letter. His name was written in a flowing script, the kind that you only saw on important documents like the Declaration of Independence.

Weird.

Not wanting to wait any longer, he ripped open the envelope and took out a single sheet of paper. On it, was a short note that read-

Dear Michael,

We have finally found you. After years of tireless work by myself, and many others, we can now confirm that you are indeed the child that we are looking for. We will be coming for you soon. There is no need to run, or to hide. You will not be successful. Anyone standing in our way will be dealt with...accordingly. - LP

Michael stared at the letter in his hand. For his first piece of mail, it was anything, but underwhelming. It was frightening!

What do they mean I'm the child they're looking for? he wondered. *Who ARE they and why are they coming for me?*

Unable to think of a good explanation, he decided to cross out his name and write Ralph's instead.

"There," he said. "Now I'm safe."

Unlocking the door, he stepped into the front hallway. As he went to lock it behind him, he saw the same mouse he'd seen earlier. This time, it was accompanied by a large brown rabbit. Michael couldn't believe his eyes. A rabbit, right here in his own house!

"I can't believe it!" he cried, dropping the mail on the floor. "A rabbit, right here in my own house!"

Michael had been trying to get his Mom to buy him a new rabbit ever since his old rabbit, Oreo, had gone missing a few years ago. She said that if he was good enough, she might consider getting him one on his 16th birthday instead of a car. Michael thought this seemed like a great deal because he didn't know how to drive anyway.

He didn't know where he could get a cool rabbit-skin wheel cover like Ralph's, so what was the point of driving without that? You're right. There absolutely IS no point. Comfort is key, and comfort is a deluxe rabbit-skin wheel cover. He looked down from his daydreaming and saw that the animals were gone.

That's weird, he thought. *Hopefully, I'll see them again later because there's no point in having pets if you don't get to play with them. Oh well.*

"I need my backpack," he sighed. "And my jacket while I'm here. It might snow later."

Michael walked to the hallway closet to find his coat. "That's funny," he said, frowning. "I always put it in here!" *Hmm...* he thought.

"I'm sure Ralph won't mind if use his North Carolina sweatshirt. He never wears it anyway! He just keeps it in this airtight, UV-blocking, bulletproof glass display case. I can always put it back when I'm done."

Carefully disabling the alarm system (Ralph was very serious about his sweatshirt), Michael replaced the garment with a photo of the sandcastle they'd made at the beach last summer. *Maybe he won't notice?* he thought. Pulling the sweatshirt over his head, he shook with relief.

"This feels a lot better than the itchy Duke Basketball sweatshirt my creepy neighbor, Mr. K, got me. My arms don't burn and my hair isn't standing on end like it does with that thing. Brrr....I really love this North Carolina sweatshirt! Go Tar Heels!"

29

(Comments like that make me wonder where the author of this book went to college...)

With all of the distractions behind him, Michael retrieved his backpack and set off for school again. He checked the lock three times. Naturally. Suddenly, he stopped in his tracks. *What is that?* he thought, spotting something potentially sinister on the path up ahead. His mind raced back to the mysterious letter he had received moments before.

Is someone really after me?!?

He quickly darted behind a tree, rolling in the grass like a true spy. His heart began to race. (Not like a true spy). *This is a weird day,* he thought. *Where can I go? I'm trapped!*

His chest felt like it was going to explode as his heart pounded faster. It was even worse than when he went to the comic book store on Wednesdays to get the newest edition of Sneaky Pete and the Cool Brigade. And oh, how he loves that.

Okay, so what if that letter was a joke? What if it's someone who wants to take my lunch money and they find out I don't have any? That wouldn't be good either. What if it's Mom and she asks if I took my bath today? That would be worse!

The pit in his stomach felt like a black hole. He needed to get to school! Maybe he could be *fashionably* late? *What a cool start*, he thought. Making note of every possible escape route, he looked out and found that he had nothing to worry about. It was just the rabbit from his house!

"Hi there!" he said, smiling.

Man was he relieved! Michael patiently waited for a response. He'd never talked to a rabbit before so this was BIG. The Easter Bunny at the mall didn't count because he'd found out it was a person after the guy's mug shot had been on the news.

He looked down again and his smile vanished. It hadn't moved! Buzz kill. Worried, he dropped to the ground to get a better look. He couldn't tell what was wrong. *Maybe all animals look like this?* he wondered.

Inching closer, his first-day-of-school outfit became increasingly muddy. *Good thing I had Mom buy me extras. Nothing beats a green and white striped shirt with a blue collar. That's why I have at least six of them!*

31

Unfortunately, he just couldn't find a comfortable position. *How do doctors do this?* he wondered. Suddenly, he found himself wishing for one of those awesome adjustable tables. Finally, settling on standing again, he attempted to brush off his shirt, getting his hands dirty and spreading the mud across his face.

"This is crazy!" he yelled looking down at the rabbit. "I won't have a medical degree until at least seventh grade! Jerry, tell me what's wrong!" (Michael names every animal 'Jerry') He couldn't bear to lose him now, not after he'd lost Oreo.

I don't really know what I'm doing, but I'll just clean his wound, re-set his bone and bandage him up until later.

"There," he said. "Now where can I put him while we go look for food? I'm hungry, so I KNOW he is."

Realizing he didn't have a shoe box, (because that's where you put injured animals) Michael decided to improvise. While improvising wasn't usually part of his nature, he noticed that Jerry was the exact size of the large pocket in his fanny pack.

What a coincidence!

Picking up the rabbit, he carefully placed him in the pouch and pulled the zipper halfway. *Just to be safe*, he thought. Satisfied, he headed off through the woods.

I know just the place for carrots, Jerry, just you wait!

It wasn't long before they arrived at Old Man Goddard's Fresh Fruit Vegitorium. All danger seemed to have passed, and now he could focus on helping Jerry. However, as it came into view, Michael noticed something was missing. Looking around, he began scratching his head as he always did when he was confused.

"Hmmm…" he began.

When nothing came to mind, he began to "hmmm" louder hoping it would help.

"HMMM!" he yelled.

It didn't help at all, but it was incredibly satisfying.

Oh well, he thought, smiling. *Maybe this is just the wrong Vegitorium? They probably have these everywhere.*

Intending to go find another one, he turned around and saw Old Man Goddard sitting on his front porch, shotgun cocked.

Nope, this is it...

"Get off my property, boy!" the old man snarled, creeping forward. Looking more haggard than usual, he walked down the front steps gingerly, keeping his good eye locked on Michael.

"What are you doing here anyway? Come back to take the rest of my vegetables? Well you can't. You've taken them all already!"

Aha! Vegetables! That's what's gone, Michael thought. *Where is he keeping them?*

Unable to move, he shuddered as the one-eyed man got closer. The gun was scary, but that was nothing compared to the eye. (Which was nothing compared to Michael's hunger...)

So why did Goddard have one eye? No one knows. Some say he lost it in the war. Maybe, but which war? World War II? The Civil War? The Revolutionary War? The Trojan War? No one knows.

Old Man Goddard was called 'old' for a reason.

But his disability wasn't as much of an impairment as an advantage. Throughout the years since his mysterious accident, his other senses had become stronger. He was like a panther waiting to strike!

Some say he killed Charles "Loosejaw" Jenkins with the pinky finger on his right hand. I believe it! One night "Loosejaw" was seen not far from Goddard's Vegetorium and the next morning he was dead. No one looked into it.

That's why they lived!

But sometimes Goddard's eye has a way of getting back at him. As the old man advanced on our hero, he lost his footing and tumbled down the stairs into the pond below.

Whoa! Michael thought, getting out of the way. *Maybe I'll wait for him inside?*

He was really hungry so he thought he would take his chances. Checking to make sure Jerry was safely tucked into his fanny pack, he took it off and hid it behind a large bush.

For safe keeping.

Opening the front door, Michael immediately noticed the pumpkins. Not only were there pumpkins on the floor by the fireplace, but also near the doors and on the countertops.

Well I know where his pumpkin crop went! he thought. *The nerve, to accuse me!*

As he walked across the room he saw the largest rabbit's foot he'd ever seen hanging from a massive ceiling fan. *Good thing Jerry isn't here.* To the left of the fan hung a massive collection of bones and feathers that might have been the skeleton of something. Or not. Michael wasn't sure what it was, but he knew he didn't like it.

On second thought, maybe I'll wait for Mr. Goddard outside. This place gives me the spooks! It's not even Halloween yet! Quickly making his way to the door, he was surprised to find it already open.

"Thanks," he said, thinking someone had opened it for him. Instead, he was greeted by a horrifying sight. It wasn't a nice person as he'd originally expected. Oh no, it was Old Man Goddard and he was soaking wet and covered in mud from head-to-toe.

"You're not going anywhere, boy," Goddard said in a soft, almost sinister tone, shutting the door slowly for dramatic effect. (What a ham...)

Michael froze in his tracks. He knew he should probably be scared right now, but the sight of Old Man Goddard covered in mud reminded him of chocolate and chocolate was food. He was hungry! Famished!

Looking around, he began to rummage through Goddard's pantry, flinging aside his backpack. He could get it later. Finally finding something he wanted, he furiously ripped open the packaging and began to eat.

How long has it been since breakfast? Michael wondered. *Ages? Centuries? Decades? Minutes? Years? Eons? Some other form of time? Basically, TOO LONG!!!!! WAYYYYYYYYYYYYYYYYYYYYYY TOO LONG!!!!*

Dumbfounded at Michael's boldness, Goddard regained his composure. "When I said you're not going anywhere, boy, I meant my pantry too! Stay away from my cereal! Put it down, NOW!!!!" (You don't mess with a man's cereal...)

He limped across the room angrily, leaving a trail of mud behind him. It wouldn't have been a good time for hide-and-seek. Goddard would have been extremely easy to find. But Michael was too busy enjoying his meal to notice the old man, chewing loudly and talking to himself.

"I'm not used to being ignored, boy! Mind your manners," Goddard said furiously, raising his voice and shaking his fist as you would expect him to. "What's wrong with you?"

Coming up behind Michael, he paused as if deciding whether to resort to violence. Slowly lowering his arm, he smiled an evil smile. "Cat got your tongue?" he whispered. "You know, I can arrange that," he laughed, a dangerous fire in his eyes.

Startled, Michael spun around, a guilty look on his face. An empty box of Mr. Sugar's Choco Squares fell to his feet. (Smooth). Not knowing what to do next, he quickly kicked it into the pantry and shut the door.

Maybe Mr. Goddard didn't see that, he thought. *Yeah, probably not...*

But he was wrong. Goddard glared at him and growled as he gestured to a seat in the corner of the room.

Michael shuddered. It sat underneath a large, hanging object that looked more dangerous than coordinating. He wasn't sure what it was.

This guy has seriously got to get a new decorator, he thought. *Maybe I could do it? But alas, I don't have a degree in interior design either!* Sighing, he realized he probably wasn't going to escape anytime soon, so he sat down in the chair and made an attempt to smile.

"That chair isn't for you boy, it's for me!" Goddard snarled. "Now help me into it."

Oh. Michael jumped up and scrambled to help the old man into a comfortable position. *Now where do I sit?* he wondered. Seeing no other chairs in the room, he found a semi-clean spot on the floor and sat down. Then he waited. And waited. And he waited so long he began to feel uncomfortable.

Am I growing a beard? he wondered.

If there was one thing he hated more than seafood it was silence. *Maybe I should say something?* he thought. But talking to an angry old man seemed MUCH worse than silence at the moment. Finding the remote to the TV next to him, he glanced up at his captor and turned it on. Why not?

Boring. Business news, he thought as an ancient looking man in a suit came into view. *Typical.* But Goddard didn't object so Michael left it on.

"And Mr....what did you say your name was?" the announcer asked, a pensive look on his face. He was shifting uncomfortably at his desk.

"Lord Piper," a voice said, sending a chill up Michael's spine. He had no idea who that guy was, but he already didn't like him. Not at ALL. What a creepy creep.

"Well that's certainly an interesting name," the announcer chuckled uneasily.

"It's a family name. It means 'future leader of Burlwood Forest and then Earth'... in Italian."

"It does?" The announcer furrowed his brow and a long, uncomfortable silence followed.

For the first business show I've ever watched, this is certainly the worst one, Michael thought. *And perhaps the best, although I can't be sure.*

Realizing his mistake, the announcer regained his composure and continued. "So tell me, 'Lord Piper,' why should we buy your jewelry? Why is it the 'next thing?'"

41

"Because you have no choice. Soon, I will..."

"Okay," the announcer said, hanging up the phone. "That certainly was umm...interesting. But hey, you never know what's next in the world of business. Let's go to caller number two."

Goddard grabbed the remote from Michael's hand and turned it off. "We live in a world of crazies, boy, crazies! You never know what people will do next. Or what they'll do to you!" The old man's eyes were wide and intimidating.

No kidding, he would know, Michael thought.

He'd never quite gotten over his last trip to the Vegitorium. Perhaps if he'd been better supervised things would have turned out differently. But Grumpy Old Ms. Jones saw fieldtrips as a great opportunity for her to take as many smoke breaks as she wanted with her creepy boyfriend Boris.

When the class got to the farm, they ran off into the woods and came back a few hours later a lot less uptight than before. A day without a teacher would be a dream come true for most elementary school students, right? How great!

Try telling that to Tommy Snaggletooth. It didn't work out so well for him.

After a rousing morning of picking fruit, picking vegetables and picking more fruit (all under the watchful eye and gun of Old Man Goddard), Tommy Snaggletooth sat down at a picnic table with the only other kid in the class that didn't have any friends, Michael.

The boys always sat in silence which Michael hated, but Tommy didn't mind because he didn't like being called 'snaggletooth.' His last name was actually Ciabatta, but he could never prove to his class they weren't really seeing his real teeth.

They were actually seeing the werewolf teeth he had worn the previous Halloween! No matter of prying, pulling, pushing, hacking, whacking, smacking, biting, gnawing, jawing, or even guffawing could get them off. They were stuck!

I mean, he didn't mind how they looked, but they DID made it pretty hard to eat. That's why he had his mom carefully pack him a special lunch every day.

(A word of caution...fake teeth do not require glue. Seriously, take my word for it)

Since Tommy had a hard time eating some of his favorite foods like Snappy's Colorful Rainbow Chips and Mr. Sugar's Vanilla Squares, he found it fairly easy to consume fruit when mashed into a juice in his thermos. Like any regular fifth grader, Tommy was going to mix his food anyway, so his mom saw the 'teeth incident' as a great opportunity to get her son to eat a healthier diet.

(Good parenting!)

It was on that day then that Tommy was mixing fruit juice into his thermos when he couldn't find a trashcan. Seeing an empty patch of grass behind him, he began discarding all of leftover peels, rinds and cores in this spot. Why not?

Old Man Goddard is why not.

After finally working his way through fifteen different types of fruit, including kinds that you've probably never heard of, Tommy was prepared to pick up his thermos when without warning, it was suddenly blown off the table and into 'Timmy's Space.'

While you might not think this was a big deal, except for the fact that Tommy's thermos was shot off the table, 'Timmy's Space' was actually a big deal. It was the name for Old Man Goddard's dog's house. Which again wouldn't have been a big deal either except that 'Timmy' isn't the name of the dog; it's the name of the kid who went missing from Michael's class when they went to the Vegitorium the year before. Now you're getting it. Locals sometimes refer to 'Timmy's Space' as the 'Devil's Outpost,' or 'Satan's Playground.' But in reality, the truth is a lot simpler than that and not actually as scary.

Goddard's dog had stumbled upon one of the greatest scientific findings in the last two hundred years and Timmy found out first. Because of her knack for digging, 'Smokey Jack' (Goddard didn't know that his dog was a girl) had single handedly discovered the largest collection of dinosaur bones in the world. The world!

Timmy Whitebread instantly became the lucky recipient of one of the collection's most unique bones when he was forced to eat in Jack's doghouse by the class bully, Jasper 'Big Boy' Clemmons.

Little did 'Big Boy' know that when Timmy discovered the rare ginormisaurus skull, he would become the country's first ten-year old billionaire. Awesome, right? After selling the rare piece to a museum, Whitebread's parents felt that it wouldn't be safe to return to the spot of their son's discovery so they moved to a remote island never to be heard from again. But how all these events, as well as the subsequent press coverage, six film deal and 'Timmy Whitebread, Boy Archaeologist' cartoon show didn't lead anyone else to the location of the bones remains a mystery. They're still looking for Timmy.

Back to today. To Michael, those memories felt like they were from an entirely different life. He was old now. Sixth grade.

And this may be as old as I get, he thought looking up at Goddard and the gun. But the old man wasn't angry anymore like Michael thought he was. He was crying.

(Gross)

Startled, Michael tried to think of something to say. He considered himself to be pretty good with people, but he didn't have too much experience because everyone ignored him. Makes things difficult. Maybe this was his chance! Gathering all the courage he could find, he opened his mouth, but no sound came out.

Frustrated, he tried again, but this time he sounded more like someone would if their foot was stuck under a golf cart.

Old Man Goddard looked up. He gazed at Michael with a look of complete despair.

"It's gone! It's all gone!" he wailed, knocking over the lamp beside him. Flailing about in his chair, Michael was unsure of whether he should perform CPR on the old man. Probably not, but you never know.

"You look guilty," Goddard snapped. "Where are my vegetables?!" he screamed, jumping out of his chair in a way that was far too nimble for a man his age. Still fuming, he slowly began advancing on Michael. "I tell you boy. At first, I thought that it was a fox, or maybe even a minotaur that took them. I never pegged you for a criminal mastermind, but that's exactly why I think you did it! Tell me, where were you on the night of August 14th?"

August 14th....August 14th... The date sounded so familiar that even Michael began to think he was guilty. Then it hit him! That was the night of his huge birthday party! Or rather, the night he'd planned a huge party for.

Oh good, he thought. *I didn't think I'd steal something anyway. I wonder if Mr. Goddard was the one who wrote that mysterious note? This must be a big misunderstanding!*

He was about to speak when he paused, suddenly upset. What if Mr. Goddard became angry HE hadn't been invited to the party? Then he might be REALLY mad. So instead of telling the old man the truth, he did what he thought any sensible person in his position would do.

He lied. (I don't recommend it)

"That was the night I traveled to the secret lair of the Super Evil Bath Snake!" he said. "While I was taking my bath, I saw him slither down the drain. I knew I had to get rid of him once and for all because I finally knew where his hideout was. Not wanting my mom to be worried, I left the water on so she would think I was still there. I slid down the drain after him. It was really hard to see down there at first, but luckily I'd remembered to bring my Sneaky Pete and the Cool Brigade special awesome-level fan club SneakLight. With my SneakLight, I was able to navigate the tunnels until I found him. Just like Sneaky Pete, I used my cunning and expertise at martial arts to climb to the highest spire of his underground castle to spy on the Super Evil Bath Snake in its throne room."

"Wait a second..." Old Man Goddard interrupted, forgetting his anger. He was lost in the story. "The Super Evil Bath Snake has a throne room?!?! But if he has a throne room...that would mean he has…"

"Minions, you're right." Michael said, pleased with his lie. "The Super Evil Bath Snake that I know is only one of over a billion Super Evil Bath Snakes in the world. They come in all shapes, sizes and colors. The only difference is the one in MY bath is in charge. The HEAD bath snake. He has wings, although I've never seen them."

"Go on," Goddard said.

49

"So while I was surveying the Super Evil Bath Snake's nest using my Sneakoculars that I got from a cereal box," Michael continued, "I noticed that my archenemy was nowhere to be found. Climbing out of the window, I carefully slid down to the ledge below, taking out my Sneakpack just in case. I was going to attempt the impossible and Sneakpack three-thousand feet down directly into the throne room of one the most dastardly and dangerous super villains to ever live. And I was going to wait for him to come to me!"

Old Man Goddard gasped. "Go on. Continue, boy."

"But I never made it to the throne room. No sooner had I *thought* about jumping that something jumped onto ME from behind!"

"The Super Evil Bath Snake?" Goddard said, horrified at the thought of an eight-year old taking on a legendary beast alone.

Having not been invited to Michael's birthday party, he didn't know how old Michael was. (Easy to forget I guess, except all the best heroes are eleven)

Michael paused for dramatic effect. Looking over at Goddard, he couldn't help but feel a little guilty. Just a little. The old man was falling for every word he said! He didn't WANT to lie, but he also didn't want anyone to feel left out by not being invited to his party.

"It was THE Super Evil Bath Snake," Michael whispered, a little spooked because his story was pretty scary. "It came at me from behind and I didn't expect it. I was no match for its length or its speed, and it grabbed me quickly, knocking my SneakPack into the depths below. Suddenly, it rose off the roof and began descending quickly, its wings furiously flapping in the howling wind. Being the adventurer I am, I…"

"Hold up," Goddard frowned. "You said you didn't know if it had wings. Now you're saying it does have wings. Which one is it?"

"I said I wasn't sure if it had wings because I hadn't seen them," Michael frowned. "Because the Super Evil Bath Snake was holding me upside-down, I never DID see them. In reality, there might have been a SneakPack or any other type of flying device up there...."

"I guess that makes sense."

"Where was I?" Michael said uneasily, sensing that Goddard was beginning to have his doubts.

That's right, my great escape!" Michael said, nervously backing away. "Let me tell you from over here. Where it's safe..."

"Ah, now you've gone and done it boy!" the old man said. "Why did you have to say you escaped? That's not how you tell a story. You have to say HOW you escaped first!"

Michael paused. "Well, I was getting to that, but...you know, I umm..."

"You're missing the whole point! You have to build suspense and doubt in the mind of your listener. Why, back in my youth I wrote a series of short stories entitled Tales of a Peaceful Town that I Visited Once in New England While it was Raining Slightly. Now, those were stories! That was great literature! You just don't find stuff like that these days. Now, it's all vampire romance and how-to books filled with obvious stuff everyone already knows."

Michael was bewildered. Was Mr. Goddard actually giving him storytelling advice? And if he was, why? Michael didn't care. He just wanted to finish the story..."

"As I was saying," he backtracked. "Did I escape? You'll have to find out!"

"Now that's more like it, boy!" Goddard said clapping his hands.

"So as I hung down looking at the city thousands of miles below, I thought back to the issue of Sneaky Pete and the Cool Brigade where Sneaky Pete had been captured by his arch nemesis, the Great Spook. The Cool Brigade was trapped in the dungeon of the Great Spook's Treacherous Fortress, and Sneaky Pete was caught trying to sneak in by disguising himself as a pizza delivery guy. (Mmm...pizza) The plan would have worked if he hadn't decided to include garlic on the pizza. The Great Spook *hated* garlic and saw through his plan right away!"

"Why that's ridiculous, who doesn't like garlic?" Goddard said angrily. "What does that have to do with you anyway?"

"I'm getting to that," Michael frowned. "Proving he's the most cunning superhero ever, Sneaky Pete lured

The Great Spook onto the roof by promising him he had the right pizza in his helicopter. Clever if you ask me. Especially since you and I know Sneaky Pete didn't have his SneakCopter with him. When they got to the roof, Sneaky Pete broke free and jumped onto his oversized bald eagle, Jefferson. Using the element of surprise, they were able to apprehend The Great Spook and rescue the Cool Brigade from the dungeon below."

Goddard's expression hardened as Michael paused to breathe. "You should go ahead and finish your story boy, or start running," he said bluntly, reaching for his shotgun. "I want to know how you couldn't have taken my vegetables!"

The magnitude of the situation was not lost on Michael. He wasn't sure what was going to happen next, but he pegged Goddard as the kind of guy who didn't like happy endings.

"So when the Super Evil Bath Snake grabbed me, I remembered what Sneaky Pete had done and screamed to distract him. Bewildered, the Super Evil Bath Snake loosened his grip and I broke free, diving into the depths below. It wasn't until right before I hit the pavement that I remembered. Hey wait... I don't have an oversized eagle!

No one was coming to save me. In his confusion, the Super Evil Bath Snake flew into a passing jetliner, his wings caught in its twin engines and he died too."

Old Man Goddard scratched his head, trying to make sense of what he'd heard. *The boy is lying!* he thought. A sinister sneer crept from one side of his mouth to the other, slowly. He chuckled. Then he chuckled again. And when he got to the third chuckle his laughter had transformed into a full-blown maniacal fit.

Holy crow! Michael bolted for the door. He'd never seen the old man happy before so something was definitely wrong.

Goddard rushed across the room to block Michael's escape, gun in hand. He wanted his vegetables back and he was prepared to go any lengths to get them. Violent lengths. He just had to do what he had been told.

Stick with the plan, the old man thought.

Being further from the door, Michael had to navigate the maze of strange objects. Despite his weight and general lack of physical fitness, he'd almost beaten Goddard outside when he tripped over a set of astrology charts. Seeing that Michael had no chance of escape, the old man began to laugh again, this time much louder. "I've got you now boy," he said quietly, apparently switching tones. "Do you hear that? There's no way out! I'm going to get my vegetables back and you're going to tell me where you took them!"

As he advanced on Michael, Goddard noticed the boy slipping something into his pocket. It was his retainer. Michael's retainer. But Goddard didn't know that.

He must have found more of my food, the old man thought. *I'm going to send his mother a bill. They told me it might be hard to manipulate him, but this is expensive!*

Standing over Michael, Goddard looked taller than the tallest tree in an evergreen forest. Super tall! For such small man, his stature increased significantly with the presence of a gun. Which you know, makes sense.

"There's no use hiding your face, boy. I can tell guilt a mile away," he sneered. "In fact, your mother probably knows about this, I bet! Oh yes. She's probably already called the police! You might even have to spend the night in jail. No inmate will be worse than you, I suspect! It takes a hardened criminal to steal from an old man. But it takes someone with no soul, a shell of a man, to steal a man's livelihood. That's what you've done here, boy. And at such a young age too, what a pity!"

Goddard smiled. *I'll have my farm back by the rainy season, they promised! It's the boy who should be worried.* Michael was in his grasp and all he had to do was squeeze!

"But that's not the half of it, you know?" he continued. "I wouldn't be worried about jail if I were you, oh no. I would be worried about when you get home! What do you think your mother will do when she finds out you lied to me? What do you think she'll do when she finds out you skipped school?"

Michael turned over, a look of complete horror on his face. Goddard knew he'd said the right thing.

"I lied," Michael said sadly. "I didn't defeat the Super Evil Bath Snake. I just didn't want you to think I'd stolen your vegetables. I'm sorry..." he trailed off at the end. He desperately wanted to tell Goddard about his birthday party, but he didn't want to make him any madder than he already was. He just wanted to help Jerry and get out of there.

"Then where exactly WERE you the night my vegetables were stolen?" Goddard said.

Michael didn't hesitate this time around. "August 14th was the day of my big birthday party. I invited all of my friends and family over and we were supposed to eat cake and ice cream. No one came though so I ate it all by myself. I didn't want to tell you because I didn't want you to be mad that I didn't invite you."

Goddard laughed. *Everything is going according to plan,* he thought. Lowering his gun, he addressed the boy in his kindest tone possible.

"Mad? Why would I be mad? Obviously, I understand a boy of your popularity can't invite everyone to his party. Why, after all, you're the 'big man in town!'"

Michael wasn't sure if this was directed at his weight, but he felt flattered anyway.

"I can't believe no one came though, what a pity! What a pity. How about this? If you go into the forest and find whoever or whatever took my vegetables and bring them back, why I'll attend your birthday party next year! In fact, I'll attend your birthday parties every year until you die!" *Which will be soon...*

Michael thought this seemed like a good deal even though he might have to share his cake. "I'll do it," he said standing up. "I don't know where your vegetables are, but I don't want to spend my birthday alone anymore either."

"Wonderful!" Old Man Goddard said happily. "Go catch that minotaur!"

This was a new start for Michael. The start of an adventure!

After saying goodbye, Michael retrieved Jerry from behind the bush and began his journey. He had no idea what he was in store for, but he was excited to see what would happen next.

Hey, it could be anything. He'd just been kidnapped by the town bully and lived to tell about it. The creepy note he'd gotten was just part of a big misunderstanding and now he was going into the forest alone. What had gotten into him!

Suddenly, Michael realized he'd left his backpack in Old Man Goddard's house. He would just have to get a new one, misunderstanding or not. He figured he'd be in big trouble when he got back home anyway so having to get a new backpack wasn't a big deal. Maybe now he could get one that would match his favorite shirt?

For the first time ever he wasn't scared! It was like the single greatest moment of his life. And then it passed.

"Do you think I should turn back?" he asked no one in particular. "I mean, I don't want Mom to be mad. She might not let me have dessert. That would be worse than not eating at all!"

Jerry stirred inside his fanny pack.

Some help you are, Michael thought. *Don't worry, I won't stop until you get home. At any rate, I probably shouldn't go home because Aunt Edna's coming over for dinner. The last time she violated her parole, the cops came and I didn't get dessert anyway. I cried for a whole week!*

He shuddered at the memory, thinking he might stay away longer just in case. The thought of dessert made him hungry again though.

Remembering he was on a farm, he sped up to the top of the hill and looked around to see if Old Man Goddard had any strawberries left. They were practically award winning they were so good!!! Well, they actually would be award winning, but they never made it to the final judging at the fair because someone always stole them.

It's probably the Bath Snake, but I don't know how he does it, Michael thought. *Then again, how does Aunt Edna get so many? She's incredible, but not in a good way.*

Every year before the county fair, Aunt Edna brings by buckets of strawberries to Michael's house. And every time he tries to savor them, she insists he "eat them quickly to destroy the evidence." Whatever that means.

Looking over to where the strawberry patch usually was, his heart sank. *Junk, nothing! I better find this minotaur quickly before I die of starvation. And he better not have eaten all of the strawberries because he doesn't know who he's messing with!*

Trying to get his mind off food, Michael looked up to see how close he was to the forest. Unfortunately, he was a lot closer than he thought!!!!!!! He wasn't ready!!!! Before he could change directions he walked right into an enormous mountain.

What?!?! Where'd that come from? he thought. *They shouldn't put things like that in the way.*

Shaking his head, he found himself staring up at Charley's Knob. It was huge!

Charley's Knob is the second tallest point in town behind the hat at Sombrero Sid's Taco Hacienda. Michael had never been there before because it was where the 'bad kids' hung out. Or at least ones with friends. That wasn't him. He stared up in awe, his mouth hanging open. But it wasn't the unique structure of the rock that caused him to gasp. And it wasn't the enormous dragonfly that flew into his mouth either.

It was his brother Ralph standing with Grumpy Old Ms. Jones at the top of the knob.

Now, you have to admit you'd probably be a little confused too if you saw your brother hanging out with your evil teacher. I mean, sketch, right? Michael froze, unable to move or speak.

What's going on? Like seriously? he wondered.

Suddenly, Michael heard a low rumbling in the distance. He craned his neck, trying to figure out where the sound was coming from. He ruled out in front of him because that's where the mountain was. *Maybe it's my stomach?* he wondered. *I didn't realize I was so hungry. Maybe it's below me?* he figured. *Nah, we don't get earthquakes here.*

The sound was almost deafening when he realized it was right behind him! He turned around just in time, to see Boris, Grumpy Old Ms. Jones' boyfriend, driving up in a rusty old VW van.

That's funny, he thought. *I always pegged him as a scooter guy. Then again, I had no idea he liked red either!*

The van that Boris was driving was nothing like Michael had ever seen before. Not only was it bigger than any factory standard model, but it was custom-built to look like a lobster, enormous claws and all. (Amazing!)

Old and beaten down, it's no wonder that it hadn't made MORE noise driving up. Michael stepped out of the way to let Boris pass, but instead the van stopped.

"Michael, how's it going my big man?" Boris said leaning out the window onto one of the claws. "What are you up to bro? Looking for the ladies?"

Michael didn't know what to say. It's not that he wasn't pleased Boris had acknowledged him. In fact, it was much better than being run over. But Boris had NEVER talked to him before. He wasn't even sure Grumpy Old Ms. Jones had. Still in shock, he stared blankly.

"It's cool dude, I understand. She is a really sweet ride," Boris said rubbing the side of his van just a little too long. "This baby is what my band uses when we go out on tour. I sleep in it in the woods when we're in town. Are you in a band, Michael? It's really cool to be in a band."

Michael smiled. "I'm in band at school."

"Not that kind of band," Boris laughed. "That's not cool at all! But that's okay bro, everybody has to start somewhere. Like take me for instance. I wasn't born this cool! It took me years to grow a mustache this thick. And I didn't get to be the bass player of the Cool Lobsters for nothing. I paid my dues man. I spent six years waiting tables at Sombrero Sid's to buy this van. Once I finally had it they let me in no problem. The rest is history dude. So don't worry, if you work hard and stay in school you can end up just like me!"

Michael shuddered. He *liked* band. And it would probably take him *at least* six years to grow a mustache with that kind of volume. Maybe longer...

"I get it bro, you're shy. Hey, but I can tell that deep inside you rock. And anyone who's that cool would wash my van for me for free while I go do something else, right? What do you say, Michael? You're cool, aren't you?"

(Right...)

Eager to win Boris' approval, Michael nodded vigorously. *I can't believe this is happening to me,* he thought. *This is the best day since yesterday!*

"I knew you would come through bro! Just give it a scrub, a wax, and drive her up to me when you're done," Boris said tossing the keys in Michael's direction. Careful not to slam the door of the car, he started to scale the cliff-side instead of taking the clearly marked path.

"Wait a minute," he said pausing. "Can I have that sweatshirt? North Carolina is my favorite team. Call me what you want, but I'm not a bandwagon fan. They're just the best. I'm the best too so I can appreciate it."

"Ummm...sure?"

"Leave it in the van! Thanks braaaa!"

Michael stared in awe as Boris disappeared up the cliff side. *He's so much cooler than I thought. I don't know why I didn't like him before.*

Left alone with his thoughts and his mean teacher's hippie boyfriend's keys, he started to look around for water to wash the car with. Reaching into his fanny pack, he found the bottle of water he'd been saving for his trip.

I really need this, but Boris' car does look bad. Maybe it'll rain and I can catch the drops on my tongue!

(Good thinking)

His decision made, he began squeezing the bottle over the creepy antennae attached to the hood. *I hope this is enough*, he thought. Frightened, he decided he was done. Stepping back to admire his work, he saw that Boris had already made it to the top.

I better get him his van back. I don't want him mad at me, he thought. *He's probably looking for it right now!*

The van's door creaked as he opened it slowly.

Oh wait, the wax! Michael took some wax paper out of his fanny pack and rubbed it over the car.

"There," he said, sitting down and slamming the door shut. Michael peered out the window, leaning on the claw to see if anyone had heard him. *Hmmm...no one. Good*, he thought.

But even if someone HAD heard him, it wouldn't have been his biggest problem. Wilma was. And Wilma was Boris' fifteen-foot python in the backseat!!!

Turning the key, Michael willed the van to start. But the beaten-down old lobster didn't want to cooperate.

Great, he thought. *I'm eleven and I can't even drive. It's probably because I don't have a snazzy steering wheel cover like Ralph.* Suddenly, he heard a low hissing sound. *Finally, it's starting up*! But he wasn't so lucky.

Before he had time to think, Wilma lunged at him from behind. Screaming, he turned the key, this time starting the van. As he flailed around erratically trying to get away from the snake, he hit the parking break, knocking it loose. Grabbing the wheel, he spun it around trying to knock the snake away from him. He kicked the pedals below as Wilma slithered onto his lap.

This could be a really cool experience if there wasn't a giant snake on me, he thought.

But things weren't that bad. Before he knew it, he'd made it to the top of Charley's Knob, safe and sound. Not to beat a dead horse, but impressive, right? Recognizing his snake, Boris walked over smiling.

"I see you've met Wilma, bro! What do you think?" he asked. "Almost as cool as my van, right?"

Michael froze, feeling Wilma begin to wrap around him and squeeze. Boris didn't even notice. He was really glad that he didn't have on Ralph's sweatshirt anymore. The snake might mess it up! (Not that giving it away isn't messing it up for Ralph in a sense...)

"At one point, we were going to change our name to the Cool Pythons in her honor, but it was already taken by some band in Japan," Boris said sadly. "That and our van already looked like a lobster. The body work alone would have been a fortune! But, bro, that was some of the craziest driving I've ever seen! You HAVE to be more careful man, this van is one-of-a-kind!"

Boris walked over and pulled the snake off Michael, putting it on his own shoulders. It would have been a strange sight had it been anyone else, but Wilma looked right at home. So did Boris.

(Probably because he lived in the van)

Michael climbed out of the car and saw Ralph laughing at him. Stupid Ralph. But what caught his eye most wasn't his brother. It was his piano teacher, Miss Dandelion, standing next to Ralph!

"Oh Michael," she said. "Are you okay? I can imagine you're quite spooked after all that! It's a good thing you're such a brave boy. I don't think anyone else could have handled it."

Ralph rolled his eyes. Michael blushed. He'd been working up the courage to ask her out on a date for at least five years. He just couldn't do it! What if she didn't like younger men?

Glancing around, he became confused at the group gathered before him. *Why are they together? And why are they playing badminton?* His heart was beating quickly in the presence of Miss Dandelion. But before he could ask, Grumpy Old Miss Jones spoke.

"I bet you're wondering what we're all doing here together. We're playing badminton!" she said happily.

I knew that.

"You see, Boris and I wanted to come to Charley's Knob this afternoon after school and needed two more people to play doubles.

It's already AFTER school?

"Your brother Ralph still owes me for those good grades from my history class a few years ago so I asked him to come along. Naturally, I invited my sister. She's the best badminton player I've ever seen!"

Michael did a double-take. *Miss Dandelion is Ms. Jones' sister? But she's like half her age!* Suddenly, he questioned everything about his life. Except, his love.

"Wait a second," he said. "But Miss Dandelion can't be your sister. You're like a hundred years old! I mean, she's really nice looking for an older woman, and you're just plain scary. How can you be related? And how do you know my name?"

Grumpy Old Ms. Jones laughed. "Why Michael, I'm not a hundred, I'm only 25! And Miss Dandelion just isn't my sister, she's my *older* sister. I'm sure she appreciates your compliment though. That was very nice of you to say that."

"It's because I love her!" Michael blurted out. "Wait, you know my name?"

"I've always known your name, Michael," Ms. Jones said, avoiding a potentially uncomfortable silence. "Why would you ask a question like that?"

"But you never say anything to me! You never call my name during roll! You don't ask me questions. All my papers come back ungraded. I didn't think you knew I was in your class? I've been in your class since forever. You're not even mad that I missed school today!"

"Quite the contrary Michael, of course I know who you are!" she smiled. "You're a very smart boy. In fact, you're my best student. Miss Dandelion and I talk about you ALL the time!"

What? I wonder what Miss Dandelion says about me? he thought, blushing.

"But it's frustrating sometimes to have a child of your potential in my class," Ms. Jones continued. "I didn't know how to challenge you so Boris suggested I give you a different kind of challenge. Why not give you the character building treatment he had at boarding school in Germany? Baron Von Quiggley is world-renowned for his methods! Sure, he might have been tough, but he made Boris into the man you see today."

Great.

"While some parents might disagree with the permanent mental anguish that neglect can cause, yours seemed quite accommodating. Miss Dandelion disagreed with our methods, of course, but as you can see, you've responded so well!"

All Michael heard was Miss Dandelion's name. He wasn't sure what else Ms. Jones had said. He didn't even know if she was mad that he'd missed school. But if Miss Dandelion was involved then it didn't matter. He would do anything for her short of getting anywhere near Boris' snake again. (Good plan)

"What are you doing here Michael?" Ralph asked.

That's a good question, he thought to himself. *I'm supposed to be in the forest looking for the minotaur that stole Mr. Goddard's vegetables, I guess. I don't even know how I got here. Also, I really hate badminton! Who in the world plays that game?!?! No one! At least I don't and that's what matters, right?*

"I'm um….looking for a minotaur." he said, knowing Ralph would make fun of him.

On cue, Ralph burst out laughing, reaching to high-five Boris. But Boris didn't high-five him back. Instead, he turned to Michael.

"What's this about Minotaur bro? We played them in the Battle of the Bands once. They were *wicked* good. We would have won, but Easy Hands, our drummer, ran out of sticks! He soloed so long he burnt a hole through his snare and busted his last pair. Minotaur's drummer was able to solo a whole minute longer so they won. They all have really cool hair. We're pretty good friends though bro if you want me to hit them up for you."

Michael had no idea what Boris was talking about, but he was pretty sure it had nothing to do with mythological beasts that steal food. (Probably not) Boris seemed like the kind of guy who would have slept through that unit in school.

Thanking him for his offer, Michael told them goodbye. Being around Miss Dandelion made him uncomfortable! That, and he needed to go ahead and find the minotaur before it moved to a *different* forest.

Miss Dandelion smiled as Michael gave her a hug, and he turned and started down the mountain. Sighing, he realized that Grumpy Old Ms. Jones had completely ignored him again as he left. At least NOW he knew why. Or at least he SHOULD have known why, but he hadn't been listening. He'd been unrealistically daydreaming about his much, much older piano teacher while she'd been talking. Oh well...

I still can't believe Ms. Jones isn't old, he frowned.

Michael smiled to himself. He didn't know what he would find in the forest, but at least he didn't have to play badminton!

The woods next to Old Man Goddard's farm were widely regarded as the most dangerous woods ever. Ever! Pretty impressive, right? No one knew if the horrible stories told about it were true, but they stayed away just in case. You can never be too sure. In fact, most of the townspeople didn't believe in monsters or anything like that all. But if they did, they assumed they lived in the forest.

You see what I mean? Michael had never been in there for a number of reasons. One, he would have needed a chaperone. Two, monsters. Michael believed in monsters.

"Great, he said to himself. "It's Chapter 10! Why did I have to go in the forest in Chapter 10! That's not very lucky..." Michael covered his eyes in fear, shaking in anticipation. *I guess I could peek?* he considered, frowning at the thought.

This isn't so bad! he gasped. *I wonder why this isn't a more popular spot?* The forest was actually a pretty nice place. Tall trees, lots of flowers. It wasn't half bad! *This looks like something from one of Mom's magazines. Really Fantastic Housekeeping, or maybe Greater Houses and Backyards?*

He skipped down the wide path, overjoyed at his luck. "I love this place!" he shouted. Michael was so happy, he began to sing about nothing in particular.

Things were really beginning to look up after his confrontation with Old Man Goddard and he was going to enjoy it! Before he knew it, he realized he'd walked so far in the forest he couldn't see where he'd come in. *That's odd,* he thought.

But because he's eleven, he quickly forgot about it and kept walking. Singing and talking to himself along the way. Soon though, it became unbelievably dark.

Maybe I should go home and try to look for the minotaur tomorrow? Mom said we're going to get ice cream after dinner so I don't want to miss that. I've memorized every special flavor for the next year. I don't want to miss my Oreo caramel mocha frappacino cement!

When he turned around, Michael began to wonder if he was already lost. Here, the big trees were bigger and the big flowers were smaller! Everything was darker. *Uh oh*, he thought. Soon he was overcome with hopelessness.

"Jerry," he sobbed, looking at his fanny pack. "What if we can't find our way out? Then I'll never get to school!"

Jerry didn't answer. Tired, scared, with nowhere to go, Michael stopped to lie down, unable to go any further.

A sudden wind blew through the forest, sending a shiver up Michael's spine so cold he thought he'd never be warm again. *Isn't it mid-August?* he wondered. *It wasn't even this cold last Christmas! Not that it ever is.*

He took the injured rabbit out of his fanny pack and pulled him closer. "You're my only friend, Jerry," he cried.

But the rabbit didn't stir and it began to rain. Despite having a teacher that ignored him, a brother that punched him and an invisible friend who had disappeared, for the first time in his life, Michael felt truly alone.

Man, this is not as much fun as I thought.

As the rain began to fall harder, Michael put Jerry on his head to shield himself. *He won't know, he's asleep*, he thought. But the rabbit began to get very heavy, and soon Michael drifted off into a deep slumber. He dreamed of chocolate and other types of food, although he wished he hadn't wasted his time with stuff that wasn't chocolate. What's the point?

Suddenly, he woke up to the sound of footsteps. Afraid to open his eyes, he tried to dream again, this time harder so he wouldn't wake up so easily. It didn't work.

Frightened, he forced himself to crack open his eyes to see what was going on. The rain had slowed down so he was able to see a clearing about 15 feet away.

What is that? he wondered. He thought he saw some kind of monster in one of the trees, but there's no way, right? *Well junk, maybe there ARE monsters here,* he thought. *Figures, that would totally be my luck. That's great. Just great...*

But that wasn't his biggest problem. It was the footsteps. They were coming from every direction!

"What's happening?!?!?!" he yelled, panicked. At least he knew where the monster was! Without warning, a man walked into the clearing in front of him. It was the organist from his church! How completely and entirely unexpected, right?

Sure he shows up here, but not at my party, Michael mumbled, disgusted at his luck.

"Good evening, Michael," the organist whispered, chuckling at his own sinister tone. As he advanced toward Michael, he was careful not to step in the fresh mud. "I trust that you will come quietly so as not to dirty my jacket? It IS an import after all. Not that you would understand what with your lack of fashion sense."

Hey! Whoa! I LIKE my favorite shirt.

"But then again," the organist continued. "I would hate to deny the boys a good fight."

Two other men stepped out of the shadows. They were deacons from Michael's church!

Maybe I should attend another church? he thought. *Is this some sort of potluck I didn't know about? If that's the case, I'm really embarrassed I forgot to bring something...*

The two men glanced at each other and laughed for what seemed like hours. It was disgusting.

"You see, Michael. Dapply, that's yours truly, never lets his prisoners get away once he finds them. Oh no! And that's what YOU are. My prisoner." He seemed delighted.

Kidnappers! Michael thought, his mind racing. *Did THESE guys send the letter? But I put Ralph's name on it?!?!? Why didn't it work?* He began to trace every step he'd taken so far, trying to figure out what he'd done wrong. *Mom always warned me about guys in vans with candy. This guy doesn't even have candy OR a van! Just my luck...*

"I have been instructed to take you to Lord Piper immediately," Dapply continued. "But I don't think I will. What that old fox doesn't know can't hurt him, right? It can hurt you though," he laughed.

Lord Piper? Isn't that the jewelry guy? Michael thought, confused. *Like the guy from the TV at Old Man Goddard's? He's a fox? Weird. I'm not really that into fashion, WITH the exception of my favorite shirt of course, so I'm not sure I'd be much use to him. Oh wait...* 'Lord Piper' must have been the 'LP' from the strange letter he'd gotten! *Why me?!? What do they want?!?*

"Well, aren't you going to say something?" Dapply said, agitated at Michael's silence. "Aren't you going to congratulate me on a job well done? You didn't even see this coming! Well, maybe you did, what with the letter and all," he chuckled. "I've been following you for years. I even came to your birthday party!"

No you didn't.

"But Lord Piper had a plan so I waited. It wasn't until the pieces came together that I saw my opportunity. I've sacrificed a lot. My lifestyle, my family. Maybe even my favorite jacket. But you know what? It was worth it. Lord Piper will reward me in ways you can't even imagine. Perhaps he will even give me the secret to his magic!"

Magic? Michael thought, momentarily distracted. *This is it! This is the moment I become a true hero*! Gaining strength from deep within, he was surprised to find out he wasn't scared anymore. He'd spent his whole life, eleven long years, trying to be special, but with little success. Since origami hadn't gained him the type of fame he'd desired, perhaps finding magic would? After all, it worked on TV. And this Lord Piper guy was from TV.

Dapply was annoyed at Michael's happiness. And why shouldn't he be? He'd devoted nearly half his adult life to this endeavor, leaving behind a really awesome job in real estate. Dressed head-to-toe in a seersucker suit, he looked ready for school picture day. His pink bow-tie matched his straw hat perfectly and he carried a cane with a duck's head on top. A real duck's head nonetheless. Whatever Michael was happy about didn't matter. It was time to act. Motioning to the Twins, they began to close in on Michael. Suddenly something large fell on top of Dapply's head, knocking him to the ground.

The MONSTER! Michael thought happily.

Furious, Dapply threw the monster aside.

Wait...that's not a monster, Michael thought. *That's Boris!* He exhaled, feeling safer already. Boris must have followed him! But Dapply was the better of the two fighters and he overpowered the bass player almost immediately.

"You think you can thwart ME, filthy man?" Dapply yelled. "Think again."

But he spoke too soon. A whole zoo of animals erupted out of the trees, brandishing frighteningly large weapons. A look of horror spread across Dapply's face.

He grabbed Boris and dragged him into the forest, leaving the Twins to fend for themselves. Sensing victory, the animals began to cheer. Michael had the sudden urge to join in when he was blindsided from behind as the Twins escaped. The last thing he remembered was a unified cry of "Long Live Burlwood Forest!" before he blacked out.

What in the hey does that mean? he wondered.

When Michael finally woke up, he felt like he'd been run over by a spaceship. Trucks are overrated. Well that, and he liked spaceships better. He couldn't remember everything about the night before, but he could remember a few things. Talking animals. And magic. *I can't believe it,* he thought. *Talking animals AND magic in one day. This might be even better than school!* But then he remembered that he'd almost been kidnapped. Yeah, the bad part.

Michael frowned. He was safe for now, but he didn't think he'd heard about Lord Piper for the last time. He tried to sit up, but found that he couldn't. He'd been trampled by a moose.

"I am so sorry. I am so sorry! I can't believe I did that, clumsy me. I'm so sorry!" it stammered as it leaned over him.

As Michael opened his eyes, he wasn't sure what was weirder. The fact that the moose talked, or well, that it talked! Unsure of how to respond, he took in his surroundings instead. He appeared to be lying on a flat bed of straw in a small wooden hut. A fire crackled in the corner, and a rocking chair sat in front of it.

Quaint, Michael thought, but he wasn't sure how the moose used the chair. It looked like it was still night outside, but he couldn't tell because the heavy rain had picked up again.

I hate rain...

He looked up and saw that the moose was still staring at him.

STOPPPPP!!!! he yelled inside his head.

He didn't want to be rude. Suddenly, he thought of something really important. He was allergic to straw!

Michael began sneezing uncontrollably. So hard he nearly blew himself off of the straw and onto the floor. That might have helped him in the long run. But as the moose's look of concern turned to one of fear, it began pacing around in circles and talking quickly to itself.

"Oh my, oh my, what have I done? It's all my fault," it said. "I was supposed to protect the Chosen One for only an hour or two, but I can't even do that! I told them not to trust me. I knew I would screw it up. Oh my, oh my, what should I do?"

Alarmed at the moose's breakdown, Michael rolled off the straw and attempted to make his way to the rocking chair. Between sneezes he tried to signal that he'd be alright, but the moose had already made up his mind. It thought Michael was dead!

"It's okay, I'll be alright!" he said. "You don't have to worry anymore!" But it didn't really come out that way through the sneezes. It sounded a lot weirder. As his face turned red, Michael tried to muster up a smile, but it hurt and he winced in pain. This made the moose go ballistic.

"NOOOOOOOOOOOOOOOOOOOOO!!!" it yelled. "NOOOOOOOOOOOOOOOO!!!"

Michael was just plain confused. When the sneezing finally started to slow down and it was apparent that he wasn't going to die, the moose looked relieved and started to breathe normally again.

Really, the moose was worse off than Michael was at this point, and it sat down on the floor in front of him and smiled.

"I hope you can forgive me, but I'm not worthy enough to stand in your presence. My name's Schumer and I own this humble house within which you sit. I know it's not much, but it's all I have. Don't worry though, Mable is supposed to come by soon. I'm sure you'll find her much more accommodating and far less clumsy. The orphanage is a really nice place."

Orphanage? But I have a family! Michael thought.

His head was filled with so many questions. He wasn't sure what the moose was talking about, but he wanted to ask him if he knew anything about Lord Piper. Before he could ask, there came a loud knock on the door and a mole promptly walked in.

"Schumer dear, how is our guest?" she said.

The mole, presumably female, was plump and wore a checkered apron. She had a kind smile and a gentle disposition that Michael almost immediately took a liking too. Glancing over in his direction, she cried out.

"Good heavens! Are you okay? Forgive me dear, but you look dreadful. I'm Mable, but most of the children call me Mama Mable. You are welcome to do so if you would like."

Carefully stepping across the floor, she made her way toward Michael. Although he couldn't place why, he felt better already. She was so busy comforting him she didn't see the moose sprawled out in front of the rocker.

"Get out the flour and make a pie!" she yelled as she toppled to the floor. "Schumer, what are you doing down there, I didn't see you! Don't worry though," she said getting up. "I'll have the both of you feeling quite well soon you just wait and see. Nothing like my three spice cider and some porlington jelly to do the trick on a rainy day. Or night. Why, just this morning, Cephas woke up with a bit of a cough, but I fixed him some for breakfast. He feels much better now, don't you dear?"

Michael couldn't decide who Mable was talking to.

I think they're all crazy, he thought.

"Oh dear, I do believe I've shut poor Cephas out of the house. Goodness me, on a rainy day too! Oh, Cephas! Come in here, you'll catch a cold out there you old git!"

Making her way across the room, Mable opened the door to find another mole, this one male, standing outside in the rain. "Sorry dear, I thought you were right behind me. Looks like the rain has let up a bit, don't you think?"

The mole, who Michael could only guess was Mable's husband, looked like he wanted to say something, but thought better of it. (Smart man) Instead, he started to cough.

Like, a LOT!

"Cephas dear, you sound like you need a little bit of three-spice cider and porlington jelly. Nothing those two can't cure by this side of Tuesday! Schumer dear, do you have anything I can give poor Cephas?"

"Sorry Mable, I'm fresh out! I was going to give Michael something, but realized I must have used the last jar when Tugley came over this morning. That old turtle sure can put it down. That, or he steals, I'm not sure which! Why don't we go on back to the orphanage, and I can take care of the children while you help our guest? I'm not very good at taking care of humans, I'm afraid. I'm just so clumsy; my antlers are always getting in the way."

Just then, Cephas, who had been amusing himself by rearranging Schumer's belongings, spoke.

"Mable, why don't we go back to the orphanage and Schumer can take care of the children while you help Michael here?" he smiled playfully.

89

Michael thought it was kind of creepy because he'd never seen a mole smile before. He ALSO wasn't sure how these animals knew his name, but if they were going to feed him he didn't really care. *FOOD!* he thought.

Mable looked down at Cephas and shook her head.

"You'll have to excuse Cephas, Michael, he's become quite hard of hearing recently. Somehow though, he always seems to repeat exactly what people say right after they say it. I would think it was remarkable if it didn't really burn my bread. Makes me mad, you know. Sometimes I think he does it on purpose, but I'm just not sure..."

Michael looked over and Cephas winked at him. Michael laughed. He'd only known the moles for five minutes and he felt like he'd known them forever. If only his birthday party had been after all of this!

He made a mental note not to say anything mean about Cephas when he was around just in case he could hear him. Not that he'd ever said anything mean about anyone anyway, but he never knew when it might be his first time.

You just never know.

"I'm so sorry dear. That's to Michael, not you, Cephas, you old coot. I was hoping to avoid this, but it looks like we have no choice. I'll find it so much easier to treat you when I have my own kitchen in front of me. I imagine Grohill is having quite the time with the little ones anyway, poor thing. Schumer dear, why don't you help our guest to the door and I'll make sure Cephas comes with us this time."

After calling for him three separate times, Mable took Cephas by the hand and opened the door. "It's a good thing we only live a few trees and a stump away, what with this weather and all. Worst storm in a century they say!"

And with that, Michael, Schumer, Mable and Cephas made their way to the orphanage. Due to the heavy rainfall, Michael would have to get a better glimpse of the village the next morning.

As curious as his day had been so far, his adventure was shaping up to be everything he could ask for. And as he would soon find out, much more.

Much, much more.

He must have fallen asleep on the way to the orphanage because when Michael woke up it was morning. Schumer had insisted he carry him the whole way which was both awkward and exhilarating at the same time. He'd never ridden a moose before, so he fought sleep as long as he could, but in the end, he must have drifted off.

(Pretty quickly I might add. Oh well...)

Come to think of it, despite how uncomfortable the moose ride had been, Michael wasn't all that comfortable right now either! Looking down, he noticed he was stuffed in a small bunk bed. He loved bunk beds, but this one had probably been made for a mole, or a rabbit, not an overweight eleven year old. *They must not get a lot of adult visitors around here,* he thought.

He tried to sit up, but realized he couldn't and decided to stare out the window instead. The sun was shining brightly through the trees. It was beautiful. So much had happened to him in the last day that he wasn't concerned with missing breakfast or another day of school anymore. He smiled. All of that would be there when he got back.

His thoughts were interrupted when all of a sudden a rabbit came out of nowhere and jumped on his face. Not cool!

He jerked to the side in surprise and fell over, the bed coming loose and falling on top of him. He liked rabbits, but he wasn't sure he was ready for that kind of relationship with one just yet. This one was larger than the ones he was used to anyway! Again, not cool.

Scared it might attack him a second time, he stayed under the bed. *At least I'm alone here*, he thought. He was thinking about how to escape, or how not to, when Jerry's face suddenly poked inside his bed cave.

"Jerry, watch out! There's a crazy killer rabbit out there and he tried to attack me!" Michael said, worried. "I think he might be a vampire rabbit, or maybe a werewolf rabbit, or maybe a mummy rabbit I'm not sure."

Jerry laughed. Michael had never heard a rabbit laugh before!

Wait a second. Jerry IS the crazy killer vampire, werewolf, mummy rabbit!

"Don't worry Michael, it's just me! I'm okay now because you brought me to Mama Mable. She fixed me right up, dude. My name isn't Jerry, but you can call me that if you want. It's Sneaks. Actually, that's my secret code name in the club. Do you want to be in the club? You can join if you want because you're a kid too and we like you. Want to join?"

*Kids....*Michael thought. *They talk too much.* He frowned. *I have no idea what Jerry just said. I think he said his name is Sneaks. That's crazy! Why would he change his name? Especially when Jerry is such a good name!*

He glanced at Jerry, still confused, but very glad he wasn't stuck in the bunk bed anymore.

Ah what the heck, he thought.

Deciding it was safe to come out, he sat up and saw four other animals staring up at him. *Whoa!*

"Guys, this is Michael. He saved my life! Michael, this is Boots, Flip, Snacks and Todd."

Todd? Michael thought.

"Todd's real name is Jerry, but those are our 'secret' nicknames."

Jerry? Aha! Michael thought. *There's always a Jerry.*

"Want to join the club?"

Michael thought about it and realized that Sneaks would probably keep inviting him until he said yes. As it turns out, he kind of wanted to join anyway. That would be really cool!

(Of course it would! How many people get to be in a club with animals?!?!)

"Of course I'll join your secret club!" he said.

"Awesome man! Let's go to the hideout then. I'm sure Mama Mable won't mind. I certainly know Cephas won't. He always tries to get us to go on club trips for weeks at a time."

Sneaks and the other animals began making their way to the door, attempting to drag Michael with them. Realizing that two rabbits, a mouse, a squirrel and a baby bald eagle probably couldn't carry him that far, he tried to get up on his own, but quickly fell down, the weight proving to be too much for his injured leg. Apparently, he had an injured leg.

Wait just a cotton pickin' minute...Did I have that yesterday? I don't think I did...Maybe I did. I don't know...

"I'm sorry guys. I don't think I can make it."

The animals didn't appear to be as upset as he was.

"Hey Schumer, come over here!" Sneaks yelled. Michael turned and saw that the moose was staring at him from across the room. *I didn't even know he was here*, he thought, confused.

"If you carry Michael to our secret hideout we'll let you join the club. Full membership, no restrictions this time." Sneaks smirked.

Schumer must have tried to join the club before, Michael thought. *I got in on my first try! I'm so awesome. He probably didn't get in because he's thirty and thirty year olds aren't in secret clubs. Whatever though.*

The moose was thrilled! Jumping off the couch, he reached down and put Michael on his back. It was impossible to hide his excitement as he began skipping towards the door. Michael, who felt quite uncomfortable already, didn't like the skipping. He was relieved when Todd blocked them. The bald eagle, although still young, created quite an intimidating figure.

"Now wait just a second, Schumer. You know how the club works! New members aren't allowed to see the location of the secret hideout until they've proven they can be trusted. You know what that means."

"Not the blindfold!" Schumer yelled, bucking Michael off his back and onto the floor.

"Ouch!" Michael said. "What's so bad about the blindfold? I'm scared of the dark, but you're not in the dark when you're wearing a blindfold. Everyone knows when you cover your eyes, you're hiding. Monsters can't get you if they can't see you!"

Schumer paused. If Michael turned out to be even half the hero they thought he would be, Burlwood Forest would be saved. The moose smiled.

"If Michael wants the blindfold, I want the blindfold," he said. The animals cheered. Sneaks pulled two blindfolds out of thin air and fastened them to the two new members. *Magic!* Michael thought. And then everything went black.

What Sneaks hadn't anticipated when enforcing the blindfold rule was that Schumer might have a hard time getting to the secret hideout without the use of his eyes. What complicated matters further was the fact that he was carrying a guy on his back who ALSO had a blindfold. Yep.

Still, Schumer's determination prevailed. He only bumped into, like, fifty trees on the way, which was pretty impressive if you ask me. When they arrived at the fort, they found that Schumer's clumsiness was the least of their worries. Two rats were waiting for them inside, having already made themselves quite comfortable. They all froze.

"You know, you've really got to get rid of this couch, it's just awful," the larger of the two rats said in a clear, British accent.

"Oh, don't listen to him, he complains about everything," said the other rat. "I'm quite impressed with your hideout, really. I mean, look at this wood here. Is this mahogany? For animals your age, you have quite an eye for decorating."

I thought rats would be you know, like, different, Michael thought.

He could feel the others staring at him. *Wait, do they want me to come up with a plan or something? Why?* No one had asked him to do that before. In fact, no one had really asked for his opinion. *Wow!*

"You know, if you like that couch so much you can have it," Michael said, a sly smile creeping across his face.

Sneaks glared at him. I guess this wasn't the type of plan he'd wanted. Either that, or he really liked the couch.

"Can we really? Why, that's the nicest thing someone's ever done for us, isn't it, Griswald?" the smaller rat said.

"It's more than you deserve, Horace! You call yourself a follower of Lord Piper? This couch is horrid! Lord Piper wouldn't stand for this and you know it."

Michael shuddered at the mention of the fox's name. *So these rats are working for HIM?*

99

"Lord Piper killed an owl one time because he hadn't fluffed his pillow enough," Griswald said smugly. "Then he killed another owl just to stuff a new one. Do you think he'd like this ugly couch?"

"You take that back, I like this couch! We're taking it" Horace said.

"Over my dead body we won't."

Griswald moved in to swing at the smaller rat as the club watched in shock. It was quite a sight to see really, two full-grown rats arguing over upholstery.

But Michael's plan wasn't done. As the rats fought, Michael pulled out his fanny pack.

"I knew this would come in handy, it always does," he said. "Always."

Reaching down, he scooped them up and sealed the bag. *Wow! I didn't know I was fast! Sports here I come!*

"You can do whatever you want, but nothing can stop Lord Piper now," Griswald laughed through the zipper. "I know what you're thinking. You're strong, sure, whatever. I work out too. But we've got numbers. You wouldn't believe it if I told you isn't that right, Horace?"

"Right you are, Griswald. And it's not just numbers. It's who's joined us that makes Lord Piper so strong. Not that he needs the help anyway. I'd watch out for traitors if I were you, Michael. Traitors! And oh, and I'm taking your couch when I get the chance."

Whatever, it's not MY couch.

Sneaks went to grab the bag from Michael, his face twisted in anger. Michael pulled it away from him.

"What are you doing, give me that!" Sneaks yelled. "You think you can just come here and be in charge? You're wrong, bro. I don't care how important you are!"

What the heck? Michael thought. *I didn't say I was important.* Stung by Sneaks' words, he slid the fanny pack behind him. *Hopefully rats don't need to breathe,* he thought. The other animals cheered and patted him on the back. *Another agent of Lord Piper thwarted! I'm getting good at this.*

But he was beginning to become concerned at the frequency of the visits from Lord Piper's agents. He really needed to ask someone what was going on. But he didn't have a chance because all of the other animals were too excited to let him speak.

"The way you captured those rats was brilliant," Schumer said, smiling. Your legend becomes greater every day! What should we do with them now?"

"Tie them up!"

"Interrogate them!"

"Make fun of them!"

"Hold their heads underwater and beat them with sticks. Then take them in our beaks and fly up as high as we can and drop them onto the rocks. Then tie them to a pole and light them on fire, parading their bodies through the city!" Todd screeched, a maddening look on his face.

(Wow...)

Not sure how to react, everyone stared at Todd who shifted uncomfortably. The seconds snaked by as no one moved. Then Todd spoke again.

"Or, we could umm....take them to Doc and see what he wants to do with them?"

"Who's Doc?" Michael asked.

He'd met a lot of new animals, but 'Doc' sounded like the smartest. He had to be! His name was 'Doc.'

"Why, Doc's the leader of our village and the wisest rabbit I know!" Schumer said. "No offense Sneaks, Boots."

"None taken," Boots said.

"Taken," Sneaks frowned. "But I think that's a great idea, Todd. You're always right. Doc would know what to do. Fly on ahead and tell him we're coming. Boots, Snacks, Flip, stay here and clean up a little. Rats are filthy. Schumer, pick up Michael and follow me." He kicked the door open and started to walk toward the village.

"Don't worry about him," Boots said. "Sneaks can be a little…what's the right word?"

"Unstable?????" Todd offered, hoping no one remembered his comment about the rats. (Irony) "See you guys later!" He quickly took off.

No kidding, Michael thought. *What have I gotten myself into?*

When Schumer and Michael got outside, Sneaks was gone. Completely gone.

Ummm... Michael thought.

Since everyone else was staying behind, they would have to find their way back to the village on their own. Because they'd been blindfolded on the way there, neither of them had ANY idea where they were. Except in the forest that is.

Still, with Schumer being a man and Michael almost being a man, they decided not to ask for directions. Why would you anyway? But it was a pretty hot day and they didn't get very far.

A few hours later, they found themselves back at the secret hideout. They were exhausted.

"Man, this is harder than I thought," Michael said. "You didn't even peek a little when they brought us here?"

"Oh no, I would never do that," Schumer said. "Would you?"

"Apparently not."

The others were gone, so they collapsed beneath a tall tree. Suddenly, it came crashing down behind them.

"Good heavens, hit the deck!" Cephas yelled diving next to Michael. "Hello, boys," he smiled.

The tree had barely missed them!

"Over here, Cephas," Michael said turning the old mole around.

"Ah, there you are! I hope I didn't startle you, but you're just the help I was looking for. You see, the Festival of the Trees is tomorrow and it's my year to be in charge. Seems like I'm always in charge, but I guess that's what happens when your wife's on the committee! Anyway, I need you boys to help me with this. You can't celebrate trees without trees. They're the most important part of the ceremony."

Makes sense I guess, Michael thought. *I mean, maybe. That's probably why he has that giant chainsaw. Wowsers, is that chainsaw big!*

"So like...why do you guys celebrate the trees anyway?" he said. "I mean, they're cool and all, but like..."

"The trees are everything to us," Schumer said with great reverence. "They're our home. Some even say they have magical powers, which is why we can talk. I've heard most animals can't talk, is that true?"

Michael nodded. It was the second time in the last few days he'd heard about magic. That was a good sign. A very good sign. Power was within his grasp!

Schumer looked astonished. "That must be terrible!" he said hanging his head. "I couldn't imagine going five minutes without talking!"

And I couldn't imagine going five minutes without hearing your voice, Michael chuckled.

(Or, yours...)

"Anyway," Schumer continued. "No one really believes the trees are magic. Most people just like them."

"That's a pretty good reason," Michael said, frowning. "Do you believe the trees are magic?" He just couldn't shake the idea of discovering magic. It was too cool to drop.

"I used to..." Schumer said, pausing. "But...I don't know, it's not important."

"What do you mean?"

"It's just that growing up I always wanted to believe that there was magic. It's so much easier when you're a child, no offense."

"None taken, I'm in middle school now," Michael said proudly.

Schumer laughed. "But you know...You grow up and things are different. You have your doubts. It's not that I don't want to believe in magic, but sometimes it's just hard to. If there was magic, why are things the way they are? Why don't people use it for good?"

Michael's heart sank. *How am I going to become a wizard if there's no magic?*

"But don't worry about it," Schumer said, seeing the frown on Michael's face. "Just enjoy the festival. No one around here believes in magic anymore so it shouldn't be a problem. The only ones who did left with Lord Piper."

Lord Piper?!?! WHAT?!?!?! Michael couldn't stand it anymore. The fox's name had come up more times than he could count. There was something the villagers weren't telling him. He was about to say something when Cephas, who had been busy cutting down trees again, turned toward them. His blade was whirling dangerously close to Michael's face. He jumped back as the mole started to spin around, presumably to find more things to cut down.

Well, that's....one way to chop trees, he thought. Frightened, he looked at Schumer who shook his head and motioned for them to leave.

"I hate to bother you boys," Cephas said stopping them. "But can one of you point me in the right direction? I only need five more trees, but I can't seem to find any! They're all gone!"

Michael could see why. Cephas had cut down almost everything around them! *Efficient*, he thought. *But I still don't understand why they celebrate trees by cutting them down.*

He turned, but didn't see Schumer. The moose was hiding behind the last tree. Not the safest spot at the moment, you know, with Cephas having the chainsaw. (No, not really)

"Should we help him?" Michael asked.

"Well sure," Schumer said. "That's what we're doing! The best help we can give is to stay out of his way. Let's go!"

Michael couldn't argue with that. (I don't think I could either) Since they still didn't know which way to go, they decided the best thing to do would be to go where Cephas wasn't.

Hoping that running faster would get them to the village sooner (which usually works, except when you don't know where you're going), Michael and Schumer took off at full tilt through the woods. Apparently, Michael's leg was better.

They laughed as they ran, exhilarated by their brush with death. After all, anything had to be better than helping a blind mole cut down trees. They weren't lumberjacks and they certainly had no intention of being headless lumberjacks! Seems like good reasoning. Michael had a severe lack of plaid in his wardrobe too.

That would NEVER do.

As tends to be the case when most people drive, Michael and Schumer weren't paying attention to where they were going. They weren't texting, or talking on the phone, but they WERE so distracted that they collided with a frail looking turtle.

Being a sturdy boy, Michael hit the animal with the force of a fighter jet and the turtle careened into a nearby pond. (Oops) Schumer would have stopped in time except for a giant root sticking out of the ground. He tripped into Michael, knocking them both into the water after the turtle.

"Oh my goodness, oh my goodness! You've killed him, you have! And right before the prophecy comes true. Oh, what am I going to do now? What am I going to do? Oh my goodness! He'll never get to meet him."

Michael shook the mud out of his ears. *What is it with prophecies and legends and stuff around here? If there's cool stuff going on I want to know what it is! Why won't anyone tell me?* He looked over and saw that Schumer was still struggling in the water.

"Help! Help! I can't swim. This is the end! Help! Drowning moose! Help!"

Michael sighed. It was pretty funny, but kind of ridiculous. Since the water was only two feet deep, the eight-foot moose was barely under, if at all. Still, being the helpful guy he was, Michael reached out a hand and pulled

Schumer to land. *Now where did that other voice come from?*

"He's gone. He's gone forever!" it wailed. A small porcupine was crying at his feet.

*Man, everyone here is really depres*sing, Michael thought. *This is really beginning to kill my adventure.*

He looked up just in time to see a hideous beast rising out of the mud.

"Who knocked me down? Answer me!?!?" it yelled. "Answer me?!?! Do you know who I am?" It was the old turtle.

Junk, Michael thought.

But the porcupine couldn't have been happier. He ran up and gave the turtle the biggest hug he'd ever seen. *Whoa,* Michael thought. The turtle glared at him and the porcupine stopped. As you can imagine, porcupine hugs aren't all that great. But the turtle wasn't the hugging type anyway.

"I'm talking to you. I said do you know who I am?" it yelled at Michael. "That's a question, boy, don't you know one when you hear it?"

111

Yeah, but you're mean.

"Schumer, is that you? You oversized coat rack, what's wrong with your tubby friend?"

Michael didn't like this turtle. He didn't like him one bit. *I'm not tubby…I just like dessert*, he thought. But since he DID know what a question was he figured he should answer it.

"I'm really sorry sir. But I don't actually know who you are. You see, I'm new here. My name's Michael."

When he heard Michael's name, the turtle paused like he was going to say something nice. But he didn't. Instead, he laid it on thick. Or thickly.

"Michael? THE Michael? Why you of all people should know who I am! You're not Michael. You're a spy. A spy, I say. A spy of Lord Piper! Grohill? Seize him!" Its wrinkly green skin was turning red.

What else is new? Michael thought.

He didn't understand why everyone knew who he was. At first he had thought it was pretty cool, but then it had become kind of creepy. Everyone talked about him like he was important, but he didn't feel important, just attacked. Super attacked. It was like there were all these assumptions about what he knew and expectations about what he would do. It was kind of overwhelming!!! He hated to admit it, but he didn't know anything about well, anything!!!

This is worse than a math test, he thought. *I need some answers and I need them now, but there's no answer key. I can't just pick 'c' here. Maybe this guy can help?*

"Grohill!" The turtle yelled, hitting the porcupine with his cane. "What did I tell you to do? Are you going to do it or do you want me to turn you into an oversized pincushion? Unlike 'Michael' here, I believe you DO know who I am. That means you have to do what I want."

"But Tugley, sir, what if he IS Michael? That wouldn't look very good to the council if we arrested the wrong guy," it said. "I mean, what would Doc think? He would be so mad! I don't even think I could capture him anyway, he's so...big."

Tugley exploded. Not literally, but in about every other way possible. Try to think about that. Yeah, it was ugly.

"You better run for your life, son!"

Grohill didn't have to be told twice this time. He took off running, but the turtle was surprisingly nimble for his age. Just like Old Man Goddard.

I want to eat what they're eating, Michael thought. But in reality, he just wanted to eat anything.

Schumer tried to help Grohill, but fell to the ground and hit his head, instantly knocked out. The porcupine was losing ground quickly when Cephas suddenly burst into the clearing swinging his chainsaw around wildly.

"Curious, isn't it?" said a voice to Michael's left. Startled, he looked down and saw an old rabbit with glasses calmly staring at him.

Where did this guy come from? Michael wondered. *The mysteriousness is killing me!*

Sensing he wasn't going to get an answer, the rabbit continued. "I find it curious that our villagers can still find something to fight about, even when the prophecy has come true. Still, I guess I should be glad for it. It's normal."

"Doc?" Michael asked. It couldn't be anyone else.

"The one and only," the rabbit smiled. "Am I that popular these days?"

"It's just that…"

"You're confused. And scared. And you wish someone could give you some answers, but every time you try to ask something happens?" Doc said, laughing.

It was like he was reading Michael's mind. He had no idea what to say. Thankfully, Doc didn't mind. He waited patiently, occasionally looking over to make sure no one was really getting hurt. Cephas was chasing Grohill with his chainsaw. He must have thought he was a tree!

"I just don't know what's going on. And I'm scared. I don't know what my role is in all this. Everyone seems to think I'm some sort of superhero, like I'm here to save the day. I mean I am, but I'm not. I don't even know what I'm here to save them from, or where HERE is. I don't think I can do it."

(Yes, you can!)

Doc smiled. "You're a brave boy, Michael. I don't expect you to understand everything immediately. That's why I'm not going to tell you. I think you need to figure it out on your own. But what I CAN tell you is that our village and others like it are experiencing a time of great trouble. Lord Piper moves again. We've passed down a legend for many generations. One about a hero named Michael who would come from outside our world to save us. He is to have hair like a blazing fire and the strength of ten men. Michael is to be unlike any other that has come before him. We believe that you are this hero, Michael."

"Oh," he said. *I'm supposed to defeat Lord Piper? Then why do I keep wanting to run from him?!?*

And then Michael fainted. Can't blame him.

When he woke up, Michael found himself once again in the friendly confines of Cephas and Mable's cottage. The motherly mole was staring down at him, a worried look on her face.

"Do you think he'll be okay Doc? He fainted so far away from the village. He's been out a long time."

"He must be. Or we're all lost." Doc said sadly.

Junk, Michael thought. And he faded into the darkness. Again.

When Michael finally woke up for good, it wasn't because he was ready to face the reality of what he'd heard. It was because Cephas had poured a enormous bucket of cold water onto his head.

Michael sat up quickly, exasperated and wet. It wasn't just because of what Cephas had done, but it was a combination of things. He wasn't a hero! He couldn't even listen to what Doc said without fainting. In fact, he couldn't even wake up from fainting without fainting. He didn't want to face Lord Piper, but it sounded like he didn't have a choice.

"Well, pull up the turnips and make a soup!" Cephas said. "Michael, I didn't see you there. That's because I'm blind," the old mole laughed, hiding the bucket behind his back. He turned to Mable and winked.

"Now, Cephas dear, apologize to Michael and go wash the bucket in the river. You know we need that for today's festival. You can't have the Festival of the Trees without my Three Spice soup!" Mable pushed Cephas out the door and came over to where Michael lay.

"You gave us quite a scare dear. Are you alright? You look like you need some porlington jelly and crispy cakes. I wish I had some to offer you, but everything is up at the festival. I'm afraid you'll have to wait until then."

Michael sat up and tried to smile. He was weak and didn't want to wait. He was starving! Not only that, but eating might help him get his mind off of everything and distract the animals so he could get away. He wasn't a hero. It was just a big misunderstanding.

"For the love of a sunset on a rainy day, is this your bag, Mable? I told you not to go shopping again," Cephas said, coming back into the house carrying a bag that looked a lot like Michael's fanny pack. "What's in this thing, it keeps moving!"

The rats! Michael thought, horrified. He had to warn them before it was too late!! "Don't open that, it has rats in it!" he yelled.

Surprised, the old mole dropped the bag onto the floor. "Rats you say? Mable, where DID you get this? The bargain bin?" He kicked it and ran across the room. "And it's ugly!" (Michael tried hard not to be offended)

"That bag's not mine, dear!" Mable said, frowning. "I did just as you asked. You know we can't afford that right now, ugly or not. We have the children to think of! The orphanage! The children! Michael, where did it come from?"

"That's my bag, Mama Mable" he said nervously. "But it didn't use to have rats in it. At least, it didn't until this morning when we went to the secret hideout. They were waiting for us. They said Lord Piper is coming and that there are traitors in the village. We didn't know what to do so we went to go tell Doc, but Schumer and I got lost on the way back. Then we met Cephas in the woods and ran into Tugley who got really mad and wanted to kill us. Then Doc came and he told me all this crazy stuff. That's when I fainted because I didn't know what else to do."

"Now, now dear," Mable said smiling. "There's no way that's true. I know every single person in this village and there's not a soul who would do the wrong thing. Sure, some of them can rub you the wrong way every now and then, but that's not a reason to worry. No, sir. That's family."

She doesn't believe me, Michael thought.

He glanced over at Cephas for reassurance, but the old mole was pretending to take a nap. Mable frowned and hit him with her broom. Hard.

"Well, put me in a pot and call me some soup! What are you trying to do woman, become a widow?" Cephas yelled. "Michael, Mable there's right. There's no one in this village that would work with Lord Piper. Except me, of course," he said mischievously.

Michael frowned.

"Why I'm just kidding, you know I'm too lazy to do that. Schumer, come here and help Mable with this bag!"

Schumer? Michael thought.

He glanced over and saw that the moose was behind him again. *What the heck?* he thought. *He really needs to be louder or something.* Michael couldn't shake what the rats had said, but someone needed to decide what to do with them too. It didn't look like Cephas would because he was pretending to nap for a second time.

"What do you think we should do with them, Mama Mable?" he asked. Mable sighed.

121

"Well dear, I don't think we should do anything with them. They seem to be talking big, but clearly they can't back it up. Lord Piper left YEARS ago. If it bothers you, Schumer here can take them to Tugley's house and Grohill can figure out what to do with them. If we must do something with them, Grohill is the one to go to. After all, he's taken care of Tugley for five years. He can take care of anything!"

In that case, Michael hoped Grohill had survived Tugley's cane attack earlier that day. If not, the rats would be on their own. But something else was still bothering him. Doc didn't seem to think that Lord Piper was gone, so why did Mable?

"What about Doc?" he asked. He didn't understand why the mole was acting so strangely. If Doc knew more than Mable did, then he could help! But it sounded like Mable knew something that Doc didn't know too.

"Doc, Doc...oh yes! Doc!" Mable said quickly. "He left you a message! He sends his warmest regrets and apologizes for not being able to be here. He hopes you can join him at the head of the table as an honored guest at the feast tonight for the Festival of the Trees. He also hopes that you forgive him for what he told you, but urges you to look deep inside yourself to find the truth. I'm so sorry Michael, but we can't call for Doc now. He's too busy."

"But.."

"No, Michael. And that's final," Mable said.

Michael sighed. He'd expected as much, but he still hoped to talk to the old rabbit. He kind of liked the guy.

Schumer came over and grabbed the rats to give to Grohill, putting them in a bucket and closing the lid. He handed Michael his fanny pack.

"Thanks!" Michael paused. "Why does that bucket have a lid?"

"It's the water bucket," Schumer said matter-of-factly. "It's so the water doesn't slosh all over the ground."

"Or come out of the bucket?"

"Yeah, that's what that means."

"Oh, right. Can we take the bucket to Doc?"

"Michael!" Mable said sternly.

Schumer paused at the door. "I'm sorry Michael. I think we should take them to Doc too, but I trust Mable."

CHAPTER 16

Schumer disappeared, leaving Michael alone with the moles.

Why the water bucket? he wondered. *I'm so thirsty...*

If it hadn't been for Cephas' exaggerated snoring he might have felt awkward after his argument with Mable. He still had so many questions about Lord Piper!

But, as he found out, it's pretty much impossible to be mad at animals. They're so great! And they'd been so nice to him. Or at least most of them had, which was pretty good. Even though Cephas refused to admit he wasn't actually sleeping, they spent the rest of the afternoon laughing and having a good time. Soon, Michael had forgotten all about the rats.

A mistake that would prove to be costly later on.

It wasn't long before it was time for the Festival of the Trees. Having never been to a party with animals before, Michael was understandably apprehensive and excited at the same time.

Will they have party favors? Should I have brought a gift for somebody? What if they have vanilla cake NOT chocolate? His mind spinning with questions, he left early with the hope of scouting out the buffet before anyone got there.

He was too late. The whole village must have had the same idea. As soon as he opened the door to Cephas and Mable's cottage he found he could barely close it back because of the crowd. The festival was so enormous, it might have been even bigger than '4 for a dollar' taco day at Sombrero Sid's. And that was always nuts! Michael's mouth hung open.

Egad! he thought.

The sheer number of names he would have to remember began to overwhelm him. Was he really out of place here with just animals?

Nah, this won't be that bad, he thought. *I'm a party animal!* But he did LOOK out of place. Everyone else was wearing a different kind of hat! *Why didn't anybody tell me?!?!*

He began to feel kind of self-conscious, wondering if he should get some food to-go. *Maybe I'm wearing an invisible hat? Yeah, that's better!* It didn't take long before a horse appeared and tossed a large hat on top of his invisible hat anyway.

"I saved that one for you, Michael!" the horse yelled as it galloped away. The hat was floppy with polka dots and it was probably the ugliest hat he'd ever seen. *What is that horse trying to say?* Michael thought.

"Ordinarily, I wouldn't wear anything like this. But after all, it's only once a year I guess," he reasoned, smiling. He was beginning to think maybe he liked parties.

This is awesome! He'd felt good about them before, but now he felt EVEN better. *I can't wait until I wear this at school.*

Even though the crowd was big, he was still able to get a pretty good view of the town square. He was a lot taller than most of the animals there, which was kind of a first for him.

Sixteen large wooden tables had been laid out around an enormous fire which was burning a pleasant purplish-pink color. The night air sparkled as the purple smoke from the burning trees slowly made its way across the crowd. It was the most amazing thing he'd ever seen.

But beauty wasn't the only effect of the fire. It apparently made everybody loose. SUPER loose. Relaxed. Animals who probably shouldn't have gotten along were talking to each other like best friends.

Apparently, they didn't study the food chain in third grade like I did, Michael thought. But as he took a deep breath, he too forgot who he was, becoming consumed in the festivities. *I think I'll let these guys throw my birthday party next year*, he thought.

It took him nearly ten minutes to make it from Mable's cottage to the head of the table because he kept showing off his hat to everyone.

Am I supposed to be like this? he wondered.

But he did it anyway just in case. And they showered him with gifts in return.

"This has been passed down through my family for generations," an elderly deer stopped him and told him. "We knew one day it would come in handy. I want you to have it," he said, putting something in Michael's hands.

"Um thanks," Michael said. *This is the best day of my life!*

While he'd received lots of weird stuff, the deer's gift was the most curious of all. He had no idea what it was! Brown, hairy and no bigger than his hand, it was unlike anything he'd ever seen before.

He forced a smile and placed it in his fanny pack, hoping it wouldn't touch anything else. *When I run out of room, this thing is the first to go*, he thought.

But the gifts DID get better. Doc presented him with a compass in front of the whole village. It looked old, but well-preserved and had a special quality to it he couldn't explain. He was excited because at least it would help him find Mable's house again after the festival. That was important. Suddenly, the animals began to sing and before he knew it, the feast began.

Michael had been to all-you-can-eat buffets and church pot-luck dinners before, but he'd never experienced something like this. There were so many vegetables, berries and pastries that not a single inch of the wooden surface was left uncovered. Mable's Three Spice cider and tangled onion sprout soup sat in a prominent position at the center of the table and were gone before he even had a chance to try them. Total bummer.

Whatever regret he had disappeared though when he downed three slices of Cephas' chocolate chunk pie.

Food is food, he thought, smiling.

As he piled a heaping portion of porlington jelly onto his plate, he noticed something that looked like meat at the other end of the table.

Well that's a little bit disturbing, he thought. *These are animals*! Todd was tearing into the meat ferociously, glancing around to make sure no one saw him. Michael realized he was staring and he quickly looked away before Todd could lock eyes with him. *Strange,* he thought.

But the purple haze looming overhead stole his curiosity and he began listening to an animated story being told by one of the villagers.

129

"I wish you could have been here, Michael. Last year was probably the best Festival of the Trees ever. The fire was so big it almost touched the sun. I promise!"

It was the deer again. "Poor Old Cephas, though. He kept having to go back to get more lumber to make sure it didn't die down. That's what happens when your wife is the head of the planning committee."

Yep, Michael thought.

"It lasted two weeks longer than usual though. The whole town was covered with that purple haze for a month! No one got anything done around here for a while, if you know what I mean," the deer winked. "You should have seen Schumer stuffing his face with apples...even rotten ones! He ate so many he tried to run up a tree!"

Everyone at the table was laughing, even Schumer. Michael hadn't seen him come in.

I'm going to figure out how he does that some day...

Then he noticed something weird. At the far end of the table sat an old frog he hadn't seen before. He wasn't laughing. In fact, the frog was staring right at Michael.

What a strange guy!

Michael looked away, trying to shake it off. *Does he want my hat?* he wondered.

But as time went on, the frog said nothing. Occasionally, he would write on a long roll of parchment.

What a buzz kill, Michael laughed.

When there was finally a break in the conversation, he looked over and saw that the frog was gone. *Maybe he finally went back to where he came from. The land of super boring people who don't know how to have a good time.* Michael chuckled to himself. He was proud of that one.

"Super boring people who don't know how to have a good time," he laughed.

But he was wrong. Definitely wrong. As he turned back to tell another story, which was probably really funny, he was surprised to find the frog sitting right next to him.

"Come with me," it said, abruptly getting up from the table and walking toward the dark forest.

Michael looked around to see if anyone else had noticed. Apparently not. Everyone else was too busy watching a horse attempt to down a whole barrel of apple juice from a funnel.

A worthy task, Michael thought.

But seeing that the frog had all but disappeared, his curiosity got the better of him and he left the party.

This guy probably isn't bad.

It didn't take him long to get lost again as he searched for the frog in the woods. Here, it was a lot darker outside the influence of the purple haze and he stumbled forward, blindly trying to find his way around. Fortunately, he didn't need to find the frog. It found him.

"I'm sorry we have to meet like this, but it isn't safe otherwise. Unkind ears might be listening," the frog said ominously. "You see, what I'm about to give you can't be seen by anyone. Anyone! Promise me you will keep this safe no matter what!"

The frog placed an old, leather bound book in Michael's hands, looking around to make sure no one saw them. Michael could have sworn he heard scary music begin to build in the background.

(I heard it too)

"Dark times are ahead, Michael, dark times," he continued. "Lord Piper rises again."

I knew it!

"The villagers won't admit it. I say, they don't want to admit it! Well, they're all foolish! It's been far too long since this town had to deal with its problems. Doc is a fine leader. A fine, fine leader. But he can only do so much. Why, not even Orion himself could save us now."

What the heck is O'Ryan? Michael wondered. *I bet that's an Irish restaurant.*

A stick cracking in the distance made the frog pause. "Isn't everyone at the feast?" he wondered, looking around. Then another stick cracked. Then another. Panic filled his eyes. "This is too soon! We're not ready!"

Suddenly, off in the distance, Michael heard a deafening crash and screams rang out all around him. Someone was attacking the village and they were after HIM! Probably Lord Piper! A traitor must have released the rats and let in more of the fox's army. He could only imagine the pandemonium going on at the feast. The frog grabbed him by the arm and pulled him into a ditch.

"Don't move," it said, pulling a dagger out of thin air. They listened quietly for a few moments. Then everything became silent.

133

That was quick...

"We have to do something!" Michael yelled getting up. The frog pulled him back down.

"And so it begins," it said sadly, ignoring Michael's struggles. "Remember everything I told you for our future depends on it. Most of all, you must promise me to keep that book safe!" This time the frog began to leave, but Michael stopped him.

"Where you going? What am I supposed to do? I don't even know your name," he said, tears streaming down his face. He was disgusted at how cliché he sounded, but no matter what he did he didn't seem to be able to avoid Lord Piper. Time was running out.

"I must go play my role, Michael, and you yours. I cannot tell you what that is. I certainly hope we meet again, for if we do, it means you're alive." The frog paused. "You can call me The Historian," he whispered. "I'm so sorry."

And he knocked Michael out, everything fading to black. Poor, Michael. That happens to him so much! Life is unfair...

So yes, you may have just realized out that I, your narrator, am the mysterious frog. You know that because I told you that MY name is The Historian. The frog's name is ALSO The Historian. We are not brothers, I am the frog. Are you paying attention?

So why did I talk so badly about myself? You know, saying that I was weird and stuff? Well, I'm so awesome that it was all I could do not to brag. You have to understand that it's my job to tell the story as it is. So that's why I couldn't help Michael. I had to record what was happening. Someone needed to know!

When Michael woke up, he thought he was at home. (Nope) The warm sun was streaming over his face just like it did through the window by his bed. He rolled over onto something sharp and turned back the other way.

I must have been playing with my blocks last night, he thought. His stomach rumbled.

"I wonder what Mom's making for breakfast this morning," he wondered aloud. "I hope it's pancakes!"

"With butter and nice warm syrup," said a voice beside him.

"And maybe some whipped cream and chocolate chips if we have it."

"And when we're done with that, we'll have more."

"But not too much," Michael said, "because then we might not have room for lunch."

"Mmmm….lunch."

Maybe he was too preoccupied thinking about food, but it took Michael a few minutes to realize the other voice was someone else, not him. Trying not to panic, he opened his eyes slowly, scared to see who or what was there.

"Hello, Michael!" Grohill said happily. The porcupine was curled up next to him.

Golly, he thought. *I'm going to have to share my pancakes with HIM?* Now he was grumpy.

"Umm…" he said uneasily. "How long exactly have you been here, Grohill?"

"Oh, please don't get mad, Master Michael! Oh please don't get mad! I left the feast to go check on Mister Tugley at home because he wasn't feeling well, but he wasn't there! When I got back, there was a big fight going on. I was so scared, so scared! I wanted to help out, but I thought the best thing I could do was to stay away! After all, everything I touch goes wrong. You've seen that, right? When I saw you laying here I thought, hey, he's smart! He's got the right idea! So I just curled up beside you. Oh, Michael, I'm so scared," he sobbed.

While Michael wasn't pleased about sharing his pancakes, he did kind of feel sorry for Grohill. After all, he'd managed to lose an old, slow turtle in his own house. That's pretty ridiculous. He was kind of creeped out that a porcupine had been sleeping next to him all night, but he DID feel pretty refreshed. (Maybe he's on to something?) He decided to be nice. After all, Grohill's tears were getting him wet.

"Hey, it's alright," he said. "Tell me exactly what happened. Where is everybody?"

"Oh thank you, Michael, thank you! Why however can I pay you back? I've heard legends of your greatness, but..."

Michael didn't hear anymore because he tuned Grohill out. *This guy is nuts*, he thought. The porcupine was pretty famous for going on, and Michael just wanted to figure out where he was. He would tune back in later.

The scene around him looked like something out of a movie, or maybe an adventure book. *It's like a movie, but real life.* There were leaves everywhere. *And it looks like they're closing in on me*, he thought, starting to feel claustrophobic in the dense jungle around him.

Shuddering, he closed his eyes. *There, now the leaves can't see ME.* Trying to shake off the feeling he was trapped, he listened for Grohill's (annoying) voice. *I never thought I'd want to hear him again, but boy, is this place scary.* Unfortunately, he had a problem. Where was Grohill?

The forest was silent.

That's weird, he thought. *Grohill never stops talking! He talks when other people talk. He even talks when HE talks! Hmm....* A thousand scenarios raced through his head. "Maybe a Notorious Leaf Monster got him?" He gasped. The thought was too gruesome to bear.

"The Notorious Leaf Monster? Oh no, where?"

Grohill, Michael thought, smiling. "Where are you?"

"Where am I? Where are you?" the porcupine said exasperated. "I've been telling you about what happened for the last twenty minutes. Are you still in that bush?"

*Ohhhh….*Michael thought. *Well, that explains a lot.*

Getting up, he saw Grohill standing a few feet away in front of a large pile of stones. A pretty stylish necklace sat beside them. *Weird,* he thought as he picked it up. *Maybe Mom would like this for Christmas?*

It wasn't really her style, but it was beautiful in its own way. The medallion was heavy and made of some sort of wood that Michael wasn't familiar with. He turned it over in his hand and gasped. The front was engraved with a tree so detailed it looked alive, like it would keep growing if you planted it. The leaves pointed out toward the edges in a menacing way and almost felt sharp to the touch.

But that wasn't what sent chills down Michael's spine. The trunk was engraved with the head of some sort of animal wearing sunglasses. He couldn't quite make it out, but it sneered up at him as if laughing about a sinister joke he wasn't a part of.

"Whatever," he said, tossing it to the ground.

If the necklace had some sort of significance to something then he didn't want to be a part of it. He looked up and saw that Grohill was still staring at the pile of stones. Suddenly, the porcupine began to cry. Again. Still.

Oh no, Michael thought. He'd been through a lot the past few days, but he wasn't prepared for this. *This guy cries more than me and they haven't even canceled his favorite cartoon. I guess I'll just have to cheer him up! Hmmm...what would cheer ME up?*

"Hey Grohill, I saw a lake outside the village yesterday. Want to take some of those rocks and go skip stones? How fun would THAT be? That might make you feel better?"

Apparently that was the wrong thing to say. Grohill started sobbing so hard they could probably skip stones where they were standing pretty soon. Michael started to back up slowly, heading for higher ground when he tripped and fell. Of course.

Clumsy me! He had fallen over the old book the mysterious frog had given him! *Man, I forgot about that thing. I bet it's important. Golly!*

"Grohill, what are those stones?" he said with a renewed sense of urgency. He had to get to the bottom of all of this. Lord Piper. The book. None of it made sense!

Still unable to form a sentence, the porcupine pointed to one of the larger pieces in the pile. Michael walked over and was horrified at what he saw. It was a severed head!

"They built this statue in his honor," Grohill said, trying to wipe away his tears. "He never liked it, but I told him, why Mister Tugley, you deserve this statue. After all, you've given so much to this village! You helped found it! But now he's gone. They're ALL gone…"

So dramatic. Michael paused, waiting for the porcupine to continue, but he never did.

If there was something obvious to say, Michael didn't know what it was. He just didn't think standing over the statue would help. After all, he had to figure out what to do next. And more importantly...he had to figure out what this book was!

"We should go somewhere else, this place is creepy," he said. "Maybe we can go find the real Tugley? He couldn't have gotten away too far right?"

"If he's still here he'll be really easy to find," Grohill said somberly. "Have you looked at the village yet?"

Come to think of it, Michael hadn't looked toward the village yet! *Details,* he thought.

Between being trapped in the bush and being scared of the severed head, he hadn't had a lot of time to do any exploring. Judging by the condition of the statue, he wasn't sure he wanted to look, but he did anyway because it was better than making small talk with Grohill.

Nothing could have prepared him for what he saw next. No building had been left untouched. Whatever evil had come through the night before had done a great job.

Good for the evil, I guess.

The scene was ugly, but not in the good way like bulldogs are. Tables were overturned, banners were ripped. The bonfire had even been spread generously all over the festival area. A purple haze still filled the air and fires burned all around him.

I don't think this is good, Michael thought.

"What should we do now?" Grohill whimpered.

He'd never been in a situation like this before, so Michael wasn't really sure what to do. On one hand, he could run away. After all, this wasn't HIS village. He had a home! But then again, the more that he thought about it, there wasn't any place that felt as much like home as Burlwood Forest did.

Maybe I'm actually an animal in disguise, he thought. The villagers had accepted him for who he was. In fact, they'd treated him like royalty! He liked that! He knew what he had to do, he just wasn't sure if he could do it.

"I guess we should try to find...survivors," he said, tripping up on the last word.

He'd only known the animals for such a short time, but he already felt like he'd lost his only friends. Which could be true honestly. He had to find someone who knew what happened.

"There must have been thousands of them last night, the food's all gone!" Michael said. "I don't even think we'd started dessert when I left." (Michael, you had three slices of pie...but I digress...)

"A few attackers, more likely. Lord Piper likes to work alone. This had to have been him! He doesn't see animals as animals, he sees them as a way to get what he wants. Unfortunately, he usually has no problem with that. He can be very...persuasive." Grohill frowned.

"What do you mean, persuasive?"

"Well, he's been known to make people change their minds about stuff. Anything really. And good people too. The village has lost a lot of animals to him over the years. He only comes around every once in a while, but every time he does, it's bad news bears. Lord Piper has never done anything like this before though. This is evil, even for him."

The village didn't look any better up close. It was like a ghost town without the ghosts. At least as far as Michael knew. Really empty. And sad. And stuff. Michael couldn't quite put a finger on it, but he kept expecting to see something. Or someone. Anyone.

Maybe I've just watched too many movies, he thought, finding the whole idea hard to believe. *There's no such thing as too many movies....or puzzles.* He smiled. *But I just can't shake the feeling that there are probably like zombies or something here...*

Deep down he knew everyone was gone, but he wouldn't admit it. He needed to find survivors to get answers! *Maybe they're all playing hide-and-seek!* he thought. *Then again, there are an awful lot of animals. I guess if I don't see anyone that means that I'm not seeing giant stacks of dead bodies which is good. That would be super gross. Maybe they're all okay?*

But since he couldn't be sure either way, he clung to the hope of their survival and his newfound friendship with Grohill. Traumatic experiences tend to bring people closer together and apparently it works with people and animals too. Sure, Grohill was still super annoying, but Michael felt like he could kind of relate to him.

"The Fearless Band of Outcasts," he said aloud, not quite meaning to.

"The what?" Grohill asked, pausing from his search of town hall. "Who are they?"

"We are, Grohill. You and me! And anyone else we find. We'll be just like Sneaky Pete and the Cool Brigade, too strong to give up. We're still here aren't we? Lord Piper didn't take us. Why, I say he CAN'T take us!" Michael yelled. "Let's keep searching the village. If we don't find anyone here, let's go somewhere else. And if we don't find anyone there, let's keep going. The world is a big place. Let's do this together, you and me. If we fail, we can always go ask my mom what to do next!"

(I'm sure she'd be happy to help...)

Michael was quite proud of himself. That was the most adult-like speech he'd ever given. He used to shudder at the thought of maturity, but it felt pretty good! True, he'd slipped up there at the end by talking about his mom, but he didn't think Grohill had heard him. The porcupine's eyes were full of something Michael had never seen from him before. Confidence.

They were going to be okay.

Suddenly, an enormous crash rang out on the far side of the village. Michael dropped to the ground. *They're back?* he thought, fearfully. *This place is no longer cool.* Grohill shrieked and dove into the rubble.

"Maybe we should change our name to the Fearful Band of Outcasts?" he whispered from somewhere in the pile.

"Nah," Michael said, trembling. "We're not scared! We're just protecting ourselves for the good of humanity. I'm going to defeat Lord Piper!" He didn't believe a single word he'd said.

As soon as the noise stopped, he jumped up, ready to get out of the strange red-orange puddle he'd fallen in. He stood up and backed away. Even if it wasn't blood (which it probably was), he wasn't too fond of liquids he couldn't drink. Now his favorite shirt was ruined.

This is the worst! he thought. *Someone will pay..... Although it does make me look kind of dangerous. I wonder if I brought another shirt? Probably. I'm the man!*

Looking for his fanny pack, he realized he'd dropped it in all the excitement. Reaching down, he noticed the compass Doc had given him the day before.

For Pete's sake, I keep losing stuff! Maybe Grohill can carry my fanny pack for me so this doesn't happen again.

Picking up the compass, he took a good look at it for the first time. After all, he'd been a little preoccupied eating yesterday. That and showing off his new hat which was somehow gone.

What bad luck, I can't believe this, he thought.

Unlike regular compasses, this one had no directional symbols. Instead, the edges were blank. The dial in the middle seemed to work though because no matter what direction he moved it in it pointed at the same place; the far side of the village.

That's where the sound was! he thought. *This would be a great time for more of that ominous music to kick in.*

...

Whoa, it just did! Unbelievable, Michael smiled. *Aha! If only my WHOLE life was a musical,* he sighed. *That would be perfect...*

"Now that the danger is over, I think it's okay to be The Fearless Band of Outcasts again!" the porcupine said, coming out of the pile and still visibly spooked. "We don't have to go check that out. I'm sure it's nothing."

"I wish you were right, but that's exactly where we need to go," Michael said. "At least if you believe in spooky compasses. Look." Michael handed the compass to the porcupine. He gasped and pushed it away.

"Where did you get that, Master Michael? That's Doc's compass! Did you steal it?"

Michael laughed. "It's okay, he gave it me. He told me it was important, but I don't really know why. You know, business as usual around here. Do you know what it does?"

"I heard that it points to danger. But I mean, I don't know about you. Like, if I had a compass that sent me toward something like that I would probably take it back for store credit. Doc was smart, but I don't know what he was doing with something so reckless."

"Grohill, we don't know what this is for sure. You're just saying that because Tugley hated Doc. There's no reason for that! This compass is like life. Like you don't know where it'll lead you, but you just take the next step and trust you're on the right path."

149

"That sounds like something Doc would say, Master Michael."

"Yeah I don't know, I guess it is," Michael said laughing. "When he gave it to me, he said to not worry about what it does or doesn't do. He said when it's the right time, I'll know. Grohill, I think this is one of those times. After all, does the Fearless Band of Outcasts ever run away?"

"Yes! At least I do. All the time!" Grohill said. "I don't like confrontation. That's probably how I got stuck taking care of Tugley. Oh, the trouble he's gotten me in."

"Trouble?" Michael asked. "What trouble?"

But Grohill never had a chance to answer him. He was interrupted by an unfamiliar voice calling Michael's name.

(Well, close enough...)

"Monty? Monty Pumpernickel? I know you're out here, son. Come to Daddy! It's your search party."

Great. Now someone ELSE is after me? Michael thought. *And wait...My Dad doesn't even know my own name?*

"Who is that, Master Michael? Is that really your Dad?" Grohill looked around nervously. They heard footsteps behind them.

"Umm...I don't know," Michael said. "I guess?"

"Son, don't make me come after you! Cause I will!"

I thought you already were.

"...You're making me really agitated, boy. Don't make me use my gun!"

"On second thought, that might not be him," Michael said, glancing back. "And if it is, I think we should wait until he cools down. Want to go toward the noise? That seems safe."

"I could not agree more!" Grohill said, and they took off running, following the compass to an abandoned looking building on the edge of town.

It took a minute for Michael's eyes to adjust. The building was still standing, but the inside had been ransacked. It was a mess! He scanned the room to find the source of the sound (which had started again) and his eyes drifted towards the center. The pots and pans were moving! He was relieved to find that it wasn't a giant monster, or a zombie as he'd previously suspected. It wasn't even Dracula, or the bully from his class, Jasper 'Big Boy' Clemmons.

Thank goodness, he thought. It was one of the oldest, smallest mice he'd ever seen. *If he can make that kind of noise, imagine what he could do with a drum set*, Michael thought. *I bet he would give Easy Hands a run for his money. Maybe even Minotaur's drummer?*

"Mortimer?" Grohill said, rushing into the room.

"My dear old friend," the mouse whispered. "How are you doing today. Better than I am, I hope?" Each word sounded deliberate and forced. How he could have made all of that noise Michael will never know. One of the mouse's legs was clearly broken and he was covered with cuts and bruises all over.

"Morty, what happened to you? Are you okay?" Grohill asked sadly.

Sensing that the porcupine was about to go into one of his fits, Mortimer reassured his old friend. "Oh, I'm fine, just fine. In fact, I've never been better! When you've been going as long as I have, rest is welcome, expected or not."

"But, Morty you look terrible! Your leg! Your arm! Your…" Grohill stuttered.

"Whoa! No need to mention that!" the mouse smiled. "Look at you! Why, if I didn't know better I'd say that you're in for a grand adventure. Grohill and Michael Pumpernickel, what a pair you two are," he laughed.

"Morty, who did this to you?" Grohill asked.

Mortimer smiled. "Oh Grohill, you were always so curious. Who do you think it was? I'm sure you know."

"Lord Piper?" Michael said, before realizing the question wasn't addressed to him.

"I'd wager that's not a bad guess, Michael, but no," Mortimer said. "Lord Piper doesn't have time for someone like me. He's only interested in the young and the able-bodied. He sent one of his goons to do it. A pretty sharp looking fellow named Dapply, I think?"

Dapply? Not him again. Michael groaned. *If he attacked Mortimer, he must still be alive! And if he was here, he must have been coming for me! I can't believe it. A guy that broken up about mud on his suit doesn't seem like he would last very long in the woods. Then again ,I've made it pretty far and I'm not an outdoorsman. I'm an outSIDEman.*

"I know him," Michael said.

"Some company you keep," Grohill sobbed.

"He tried to kidnap me, remember? You guys saved me!"

"Oh yeah."

"What was he wearing?" Michael asked, scratching his head. "This is really important. At least maybe. I don't know...possibly, you know?"

"Isn't that a little forward?" Grohill frowned.

"A pinstriped suit with a deep purple flower on it if I remember correctly. Why?" Mortimer said.

"That's a different suit than he was wearing during the attack, and it's only been a few days since then, right, Grohill?"

"I think so. I mean, I guess so...wait, why are you so worried about what he was wearing?" the porcupine asked. "Are you in the market for a suit? I didn't know you had such an affinity for men's fashion?"

"Nah, not yet," Michael laughed. "Mom said I have to lose some weight before I can get a suit. Totally unfair! But if he changed that means that his secret hideout can't be too far away. Unless he just carries around lots of different suits which would be heavy. Maybe we can go find his hideout! If we do, he might be able to lead us to Lord Piper!"

"I don't know, Michael," Grohill said. "Walking right into enemy territory like that. It might be, you know, dangerous. I don't like dangerous."

(Only crazy people do...)

"No, Michael's right, it's the only way," Mortimer said turning to his friend. "Grohill, you know I love you like a son, I always have. And that's why I feel like I can say what I'm about to. With love. Why are you so scared of everything all the time? Do you think you're going to fail?" he coughed. "Do you think people won't like you? Why, if you're scared of life, you're not living! I've known you for years and years. I've seen you grow up right before my eyes. I probably know you better than anyone else. But you don't have to be big to do big things! When Doc was born, he had a bad leg. They told him he'd never walk! I think you've seen him do it, have you not? Grohill, I believe in you. I always have. You just need to believe in yourself."

Mortimer smiled, closing his eyes. *He must have been holding that in for years*, Michael thought. He was probably right.

"You take care of him now, son," Mortimer said gesturing to Grohill. Michael nodded.

"And you take care of him," he said, gesturing at Michael. Grohill nodded, tears now streaming freely down his face. "Oh, the things you two can do," Mortimer laughed. "The things you two WILL do! It almost makes an old mouse feel young again. But alas, I cannot join you. I think I'm ready to rest now." Or in his case he meant rest, you know, eternally.

Michael knew he was gone. It was like he felt the mouse's soul leave the room. He looked over at Grohill. The porcupine had a look of determination on his face.

"Morty's right. If we're going to find everyone and make this village right again, we need to go to Dapply's. If we can find Dapply, then we can find Lord Piper. Everything I know about this tells me to run in the other direction, but I can't. That would be an insult to Morty's memory. If only we knew where to start."

Michael laughed. "You know, you never really had a choice. I would have dragged you with me anyway. This just makes it easier. I don't want to do this alone."

"And you won't have to unless I get scared and run away."

Michael smiled. "That's kind of the problem though. I was hoping to ask Mortimer which way Dapply went, but I didn't have a chance to. Anything to get us going in the right direction would help."

Michael paused. He looked down at the compass hoping it would give him a clue. Nothing. The dial had vanished! *Figures. When I actually want it to tell me something. It's like a really unreliable car.*

"Maybe....we didn't have to ask him because he already told us!" Grohill said excitedly.

"What do you mean? Don't mess with me, Grohill, it's been a weird day."

Grohill ignored him. "Well he said that Dapply's suit had a deep purple flower on it, right? It must have been a pyrcantheon! There's only one place I know where they grow that stuff. Legally at least. Anyway, it's not more than a two day's walk from here. If we follow the flowers, I bet we'll find his hideout!"

"Grohill, that's really brilliant!" Michael said triumphantly. "We might get home for dinner after all. Morty was right, you are something. Let's go then, we don't have a moment to lose!"

"There is one problem though," Grohill said. His face turning red. "I'm, you know, kind of hungry NOW. I don't think I can start a journey on an empty stomach."

This is definitely my kind of guy, Michael thought. Remembering he'd packed some of the festival food in his fanny pack, he unzipped it and brought out two oatmeal cream pies. "Then let's not start a journey hungry. A feast of champions!"

"A feast of champions indeed!"

Michael had mastered the art of space management over the years and had managed to cram at least fifteen different oatmeal cream pies into his fanny pack. They ate all of them.

The compass was in there too, but he didn't really care. It might have been the influence of the purple haze, or it might have just been the aged apple cider they drank, but they were carefree. They had a plan. The search party had disappeared. And for once, the Fearless Band of Outcasts felt very much fearless.

Michael's head was killing him.

"Mable always said you can never have too much Three Spice Cider, but I think she might be wrong," Grohill said wincing.

"Yeah I think I'm going to die," Michael said. "I could probably sleep the whole day."

"Yeah, probably," Grohill laughed. "You want to?"

"Nah. We're out of food. Let's get going."

"Good point." They started to walk off in no particular direction. Grohill said he would have to figure out where they were before he could figure out where they were going.

"Where are we going again?"

"Grohill, we just talked about this," Michael said, irritated. He was extremely hungry.

"I didn't say that, Master Michael."

"Oh."

"Don't mind me," the voice said again. Michael turned around and saw Doc smiling up at him.

Where did he come from? Michael wondered. *What the heck? He just pulled a Schumer!* "Doc! We thought you'd been captured!" He exchanged glances with Grohill, who looked just as confused as he was.

"And I thought the same for you." The rabbit had tears in his eyes. "I'm ever so happy to see you safe and sound. How did you escape?"

"Well, I can't speak for Grohill, but I wasn't even in the village when everything happened," Michael said.

"You weren't? Were you not enjoying the feast?" Doc looked concerned.

Ah, the feast, Michael sighed. "Oh no, I was REALLY enjoying it!" He made sure to emphasize his love for food in the hopes that Doc had some with him. "But I was following this mysterious frog who gave me this really weird book. I don't know what it is, but it was super weird. I guess everything happened while I was gone."

"A book, you say?" Doc asked, confused. Grohill shifted uncomfortably. Michael hadn't told him about the book yet either.

"But I'm not supposed to tell anyone about it," Michael said. "I mean. It wasn't a big deal. The book, that is. It was just a book. I think I lost it."

"Now Michael, you know you can trust me. I know we just met, but I know you. We've been watching you for years." Doc smiled.

Like that's supposed to make me feel better! I thought that was only Santa...

(Santa watches the people watching you too...)

"You don't have to tell me right now if you don't want to, Michael," Doc said. "Where were you, Grohill?"

The porcupine looked nervous. "I was...I was just looking for Tugley!" he whimpered. "After all, he wasn't feeling well, so I went to go check on him."

"Poor Tugley. Wasn't he at the feast?" Doc asked.

"Um...I don't think he was."

"I didn't see him," Michael said.

"No one asked you!" Grohill snapped. "No, no. I can be quite sure he wasn't at the feast because I had to go check on him."

"I guess another founder made the toast, then?"

"There was TOAST?" Michael said, disappointed.

"Not that kind of toast, Michael."

"Ummm...." Grohill murmured.

"Something tells me that someone here is NOT telling the truth," Doc said glancing at Michael. *What? What did I do? There really was a frog!*

"But what I DO know is that you're both okay and that's what matters. Now, where were you headed off to so quickly when you nearly bowled me over?"

"We were off to find Dapply's hideout, he's one of Lord Piper's henchmen," Grohill said. "Mortimer told us he had a purple flower on which as you know can only be found..."

"Illegally, I know," Doc sighed.

"No, no there's a bed not far from here!" Grohill said.

"Is there? You mean the one you promised to burn down last month when you were helping me on the Citizen's Patrol?"

"Umm...." Grohill said.

"You know, you're doing that a lot lately." Doc said sternly.

"I..."

Michael wasn't really listening, business as usual. Something else was bothering him. He didn't know why Grohill looked so nervous! If he'd been taking care of Tugley, what was the big deal? That's what he'd told him earlier, but he seemed a lot more hesitant around Doc.

That wasn't what was REALLY bothering him though. He was sure the porcupine was harmless, just nervous. The hair on Michael's arms was standing up and that meant something was up. *If only the hair on my head would do the same thing, that would be cool,* he chuckled.

Suddenly, he realized what the problem was. *Aha!* Doc had never explained where HE'D been!

"Wait Doc... You weren't at the feast when I left. Where did you go?" Michael asked.

Doc looked surprised. Grohill looked relieved. Apparently, his story hadn't quite cut it with the town leader. They'd still been talking when Michael had interrupted him.

"Why, Michael didn't I tell you already? I had just stepped out for a moment," Doc said cheerfully. "When I came back, everyone was gone. I couldn't believe it!"

Right, Michael thought. *He's really bad at coming up with stories,* but *I'm SO much better. Just ask Mr. Goddard! I just don't know if I believe him...Something seems off.*

He trusted the old rabbit because that's what his heart had told him to do, but now he wasn't so sure.

Maybe my heart changed its mind? I'm SO indecisive! Grrr....But the only way Lord Piper would have been able to pull off this attack would have been if he hadn't done it alone. He would have needed someone on the inside. Something about this just doesn't add up.

"The rats were right," he said fearfully.

"What?" Doc asked.

"Why are you hanging out with rats?" Grohill said.

- CHAPTER 21 -

"They warned me about this. They said there was a traitor in the village. I mean, that's the only way Lord Piper could have succeeded, right? I've been thinking about what happened. I don't know anything about being bad. After all, I'm a pretty good guy. But something about your story just doesn't add up, Doc."

"Michael Socrates Pumpernickel!" Doc scolded, scaring him.

Michael shuddered at the use of his full name.

"Never, and I mean NEVER in my time as leader of this village has someone accused me of treachery!" He was shaking with anger. "I have given everything I have to these people, to this town. I thought you would understand. Especially because of what I told you."

"What did he tell you, Michael?" Grohill asked accusingly.

I think I made everyone mad, Michael thought.

"Wait a second, Doc. I didn't mean, you know..."

"No, you're right, you're right," Doc sighed, the lines on his face showing. "I didn't just step away from the feast.."

Aha!

"Forgive an old rabbit for trying to protect his reputation so foolishly after all these years. If you had only known what I'd been doing you might never look at me in the same way again. But alas, I fear you will not anyway. There's no use in telling you now."

"Is this one of those times where you say that because you really want to tell us?" Michael asked.

"No, Michael. I actually don't. That's why I said it. But if I did want to tell you, but said it that way it would be called reverse psychology."

Right!

Grohill spoke up. "Every spine in my body hurt when you didn't believe me, Doc. But I guess I have no reason to doubt you after all you've done for the village."

"Please tell us, Doc," Michael urged. "I can't take the suspense! That, and I still have no idea what reverse psychology is."

"I wouldn't worry about it," Doc chuckled. " But if you promise not to look down on me, I'll tell you." Both Michael and Grohill nodded vigorously.

167

"I'd noticed Tugley and Mable had left the feast so I went to go find them. When I got out of earshot of the festival, I heard voices not too far off in the woods. I went to go investigate and saw Tugley and Mable in a heated argument with a few rats. Keeping my distance, I inched closer, trying to hear what they were talking about. My instincts told me to stay away, but I was just too curious to stop. I didn't hear everything, but Tugley said something about following through with a plan. Mable didn't like it, but she agreed because it might help the children. I felt bad about spying on them, but something just didn't feel right, you know? I took the long way back to give me some time to think, but when I got here it was too late."

"How dare you accuse Mister Tugley of any wrongdoing!" Grohill yelled. "Hanging out with rats? You were always jealous of him, weren't you? Thinking he wanted to be town leader? Who else do you want to make stuff up about? Who's next?"

(Who's next, indeed?)

Grohill was red in the face. Michael thought he looked like a Christmas ornament or something. Like the really ugly kind you threw out with the tree, or put in the back. Definitely the kind you avoided. Suddenly, Christmas scared him! He had no idea what to think about what Doc had just said. The rabbit looked tired. Very tired. He must have suspected this kind of reaction. That's why he was so hesitant to tell them in the first place.

"Grohill, I'm sorry you feel that way, I really am," Doc said sadly. "I thought you knew me well enough to know I would never say anything bad about Tugley. We all owe a lot to him."

"You certainly do!"

"And I know I can't make you believe me. I was shocked myself when I heard them talking. But you must know I mean you no harm. And I would never, ever wish any harm on anyone inside this village."

This is NOT cool, Michael thought. *I don't know who the traitor is! Grohill? Doc? Tugley? Mable? EVERYBODY?!?!?! Lord Piper has already won.* He was devastated. He hadn't even been a hero for a whole week before he'd failed. He would just have to make a choice. Should he side with Grohill? Or should he stick with Doc?

Taking a pad of paper out of his fanny pack he started to make a 'pro-con' list. *Hmmm...pros,* he thought. *If I side with Grohill he'll still be my friend. Cons...I don't*

169

really like Tugley so Doc's story is probably true. Pros...if I side with Doc instead of Grohill then I won't need him as my friend because Doc will be my friend. Cons...Doc is kind of mysterious. He just gives me a really weird vibe.

"WELL?!?!" Doc and Grohill said together.

Michael jumped. He'd really been enjoying making that list. *Maybe that could be my new hobby?* he thought. *List making!*

But what had he decided?

"Grohill, you know you're my friend," Michael said. "But Doc, you know I respect you. Even if I never really know what you're talking about. You have glasses. You just seem really smart. So I'm sure you know how hard this is for me. I mean, seriously! After all, it's hard to believe anything anymore. Only a few days ago I was just an ordinary guy. But I wished for greatness and I got it! With greatness comes responsibility and that's a lot for an eleven year old to handle. So if there's any way for us to just get along and forget whatever we're talking about let's do it. We have to work together. I'm in sixth grade now."

Michael found that he just couldn't side with either animal. It was too hard. Fighting against Lord Piper was too hard. The fox always seemed to be one step ahead of him.

"Well said, Michael Pumpernickel, well said," Doc clapped. "Even if I have no idea what that last part had to do with anything! I wish there was an easy solution like you say, but I'm afraid there's not. So I offer myself to you. Please, take me as your prisoner. Let me show you my loyalty when it matters most. Cuff me, tie me, or leave me for dead. I will do you no harm."

Doc held out a rope and Grohill quickly moved to bind him. Michael hesitated. He wanted to stop him, but found that he couldn't.

I must find out the truth.

"Try to hurt Mister Tugley now!" Grohill snarled. An unbelievable change had overcome the small animal.

I hope I didn't eat whatever he had, Michael thought, although, he probably had. He eats everything!

Grohill tied the rope tightly around Doc's neck and paws. Michael said nothing. He was ashamed.

"You're right, Grohill. I wouldn't hurt Tugley. Now where was it you said we're going?"

"Who said you could talk, old man?" Grohill snapped, smacking Doc across the face. "Michael and I call the shots around here not you. And by Michael and I, I pretty much just mean me. Isn't that right, Michael?"

"Umm..." Michael didn't know what to say. At the moment, he didn't really like anybody.

Grohill hit Doc again. "Don't like that, do you? Well you better get used to it until you come clean."

I have to protect him, Michael thought. *Even if he's bad, it's the right thing to do.*

"No, Grohill," Michael said sternly. The porcupine's spines stood on end. "The Fearless Band of Outcasts are many things. They're fearless. And they're outcasts. But above all, they're NOT bullies. I know what you're doing. I really do. But hitting Doc isn't going to bring Tugley back. He means us no harm, he's already shown that. The least you could do is to pay Doc back with your own silence."

Grohill screamed and kicked a tree limb in anger, injuring his foot. This made him even madder. *It's hard to toe the line between good and evil,* Michael thought. *I'm not sure what side I'm on right now. But to defeat The*

172

Great Spook, Sneaky Pete had to make some hard decisions. He never did it alone. Unfortunately, I'm alone.

"Well come on then," Grohill said roughly, grabbing the rope attached to Doc's neck.

"Why don't I hold on to him?" Michael asked, taking the rope from the porcupine. "That way you can devote all of your energy to finding Dapply's hideout. To leading us. It's an extremely important job, you know. Not just for anybody!"

Grohill looked surprised. "But Master Michael," he said, reverting back to his gentle, nervous self. "You're the leader! You're the chosen one. I've heard legends about you since before my spines came in. I'm just…me."

"That's right," Michael said. "You are you. I'm certainly not. Thank goodness. But Grohill is exactly what we need right now. In issue 347 of Sneaky Pete and the Cool Brigade, Sneaky Pete was trapped in the fortress of The Great Spook. He didn't have his SneakLight, and his SneakCopter was in the body shop to get flames painted down the side. If it wasn't for his friend Jefferson, he never would have escaped."

"What did Jefferson do?" Grohill asked.

"He led, Grohill. Sneaky Pete had tried everything. But Jefferson knew of a way out no one else knew about. He didn't want to try it because he was afraid it wouldn't work. But Sneaky Pete trusted him. And you know what? It worked."

"Then let's go find Dapply and get Tugley back. For Burlwood Forest!" Grohill yelled.

"For Burlwood Forest," Doc whispered. And this time the porcupine didn't stop him. He was thinking about other things.

He was a leader.

Michael's mood was sour and he didn't care if anyone knew it. *I feel like those gummy worms that make my mouth water just thinking about them,* he thought.

(Those are wonderful...)

Grohill had reverted back to his angry ways and much of their journey was spent in an awkward silence, something he'd never experienced before.

Usually, I have a lot to say. But I guess I just don't have a lot to say to these guys. At least not Grohill.

They'd argued a lot over the last few days. Apparently Michael's inspiring speech had worn off. *If he'd read the comics himself he wouldn't need me to tell him about Sneaky Pete and Jefferson. Doesn't he appreciate good literature?*

But Sneaky Pete wasn't really the problem. It was that Grohill didn't really know where the pyrcantheon was, despite repeatedly (and angrily) assuring the others. Every time Doc spoke up, he would lash out, breaking the deafening silence for only a minute.

You give a guy a little bit of power, Michael thought. *I hope he never becomes school president.*

On the third day, Michael tried to talk to Doc to find out where to go. Grohill had gone away to find some berries, but returned before they finished. He was furious.

"I'm the leader now, not you, Chub Scout. Don't talk to him!"

That's offensive. And really lame, Michael thought. *Oh how I wish I'd never told him he could be leader. Worst idea ever. I was just running from my destiny, I guess. Actually, better yet, I wish I was back home instead of here at all. Even better still, I wish I was in school! Then Mom could pick me up and take me to the park before dinner as a reward for good grades. We could feed the ducks and talk to Crazy Jack. Ducks don't argue like this, they always get along.*

But then he remembered the time he saw two ducks fighting. They were down on the bank by the water and one of them was trying to strangle the other duck with its neck.

Is there no justice in this world? he thought, sighing. *My life is like something out of a really rotten book.*

(That's a rather offensive statement)

Maybe the frog's book has the answers? he wondered.

(Now we're talking!)

Tonight, he decided. *I'll make sure Doc and Grohill are asleep and I'm going to open it. The mysterious frog seemed to think it would help. He's bats, but I'll take whatever I can get.*

Just as he'd suspected, they were no closer to finding Dapply's hideout by nightfall.

Couldn't we just ask someone? he wondered.

Grohill went to bed early, still angry from their argument that morning. Michael sat on 'guard duty' while the old rabbit warmed his paws by the fire.

This might be my only chance. His back is turned!

The book was heavy in his hands and it looked so old he was afraid to open it. He spent a long time studying the engravings on the outside, trying to figure out what they meant. *In movies this kind of stuff always means something. This must be in a different language? French maybe,* he thought. *If the inside is anything like the outside, the mysterious frog greatly overestimated my language skills!*

"What is that, Michael?" Doc said suddenly.

Gosh! He shoved the book back into his fanny pack quickly, causing the old compass to fall out.

"Is that my compass?" the rabbit asked.

Michael nodded, relieved. "Maybe....It's awful though. Seriously, you got ripped off BIG time."

"Michael, you know there's no writing on the side intentionally, don't you? Like on purpose. That's not how it works. It doesn't tell direction, You knew that right?"

"Umm...yeah..."

"After all, how else did you and Grohill know where to find Mortimer?"

"Luck I guess. Or awesomeness. I just thought it was broken."

"Broken, ha!" Doc laughed. Grohill stirred not far away, but didn't wake up. The two continued in a whisper.

"What I meant to say is no, Michael, it's not broken because it's not a regular compass. It doesn't tell direction. "

"Then what's the point?"

"I was getting there. It..."

"Sorry."

"Michael?"

"Yes, Doc?"

"Please stop talking."

"Yes, sir."

"Thank you. As I was saying, it's the tool of a hero! It points toward those in need." Doc looked relieved that he'd finally been able to complete his sentence.

"Ummm, Doc?"

"Yes, Michael."

"It's pointing at us...that means we're heroes right?"

"Certainly not, Michael. Have you been listening to anything I've been saying? It means that we're in trouble."

"Oh."

Michael and Doc looked at each other in silence, the compass' warning beginning to sink in. The forest around them was calm. Perhaps too calm.

I could stay here forever, he thought. *It just looks like that wouldn't be a good idea.*

He was right. No sooner had his mind switched to thoughts about death, that a light shone directly in his eyes, temporarily blinding him. Dogs began barking everywhere. He was surrounded.

"There he is, son of a gun! Good job boys, we've found him!"

It was the search party! His run-in with them the first time hadn't been all that positive. Not that he didn't want to be rescued, but he just had a feeling that they weren't all that interested in his well-being. That and there was more adventuring to be done before he went home. He had to defeat Lord Piper! He had more life to live! Unfortunately, it looked like the living part might have to be put on hold. He was done for!

"Git 'em, boys!" the voice yelled triumphantly. The sound of dogs barking was dangerously close. They were closing in on him. Not good.

Michael grabbed Doc and started running as fast as he could. His sight still hadn't returned completely so he stumbled forward, blindly feeling his way through the darkness. Apparently the dogs weren't getting the job done because he heard the man yell in anger, although still close behind.

Maybe I'm going to make it after all? he thought. *I just don't know why the police are so mad if this is truly a search party?*

But angry didn't begin to describe the man that was in hot pursuit. He'd left his dogs behind and was running with superhuman speed after Michael. Creepy.

Somehow, Michael continued to keep his lead, but perhaps it was just because he kept weaving back and forth causing the man to continually retrace his own steps. Michael didn't do it on purpose, he just couldn't see.

Suddenly, he felt something rush by his head. It landed in a tree beside him with a sickening crunch causing splinters to fly everywhere.

Bullets! This cannot be legal! he thought, horrified. *If I can somehow channel the power of my favorite shirt, now's the time to do it!*

181

But he just kept running, it was all he could do. Strangely, Doc hadn't said anything the whole time. Michael was beginning to worry about the effect of the excitement on the old rabbit's heart, but he couldn't afford to stop, not yet.

His sight had returned, but it was still too dark to see where he was going. Bullets were still streaking by and he was losing ground. The man had strapped on a pair of night vision goggles and was expertly weaving between the trees.

(At least I think. I don't have the goggles either...)

This would be a really great time to have some SneakGoggles, but Mom wouldn't buy me the right kind of cereal that they come in! What's up with that?!? Not cool...

It wasn't a good time to be mad at his Mom. He had to find a hiding place! Michael wasn't very good at making decisions, but luckily he didn't have to. As he was rounding a bend in the woods, he tripped over a large stump and started to fall down the hill.

He fell for what seemed like hours, the leaves around him exploding with a shower of bullets. He could hear the man yelling excitedly behind him, but he couldn't grab onto anything long enough to stop his momentum. Finally, when he reached the bottom of the hill, he tumbled into a small cave. He could tell that he was hurt because every bone in his body screamed out in pain.

*I hope Doc's okay...*he thought as he blacked out.

When he woke up, Michael's whole body was sore. That kind of thing happens when you tumble down a hill. Fortunately though, the bleeding had stopped, which he later found out had started to begin with. He looked around and saw that he was lying in a small cave, hidden from the forest above.

That's lucky, he thought. *How long have I been out?*

"Doc?"

When the rabbit didn't answer him, he discovered that he hadn't been carrying him after all! Apparently, he'd been running around with a small, moss-covered log.

Gosh! he thought, immediately ashamed at his mistake. His heart was exploding with guilt. *I was so worried about saving myself, I didn't even save my friends!* As usual, he began to cry.

(That's a hobby).

Sitting up slowly, he opened his fanny pack. *FOOD will make me feel better!* he thought. But all he had was a few tubes of Mr. Sugar's Vanilla Squares. *Great...*

"I had this? Why?!? I don't like vanilla!"

Talk about dramatic. He wasn't really angry about the vanilla squares (he would have eaten anything), but he wasn't shy about taking his anger out on them either. In reality, he was mad about losing his friends.

What's the point of being saved if you're alone?

"I'll take them if you don't mind."

What? Who said that? Startled, he jumped and hit his head on the cave ceiling.

"Ow!"

The tube rolled behind him to the feet of the stranger. It was unlike any creature he'd ever seen. Tall and slender, it wore a rather stylish necklace. It was the same necklace he'd seen near the village!

Weird, but probably not significant...

He wasn't scared, but wasn't sure he shouldn't be. Backing up, he tried to find courage to address the beast.

"What's the big idea! What are you doing in my cave anyway?"

"Your cave? I do believe you're in MY cave," it said. "But you don't have to thank me for taking these off your hands. You see, I'm just SO hungry! Usually, I wouldn't eat this filth, I much prefer Mr. Sugar's Choco Squares...."

"Me too!"

"But I need to eat something. I'm famished."

Without waiting for a response, it furiously tore into the box of Vanilla Squares. Michael looked on in horror.

Those are mine! I don't care whose cave this is! He was becoming angrier and angrier by the second. *What is this thing anyway?*

It licked its lips and started to go through Michael's fanny pack to look for more food.

Oh no you don't! The nerve! But Michael stopped himself, his curiosity getting the better of him. *Seriously, what IS this thing?* And this his anger turned to happiness. *I can't wait˙to tell everybody at school!* He smiled. *I can't believe it. I discovered a new species!*

"A new species, did you say?" the animal asked between bites, having found another tube of Vanilla Squares. "Last time I checked I'm an otter. I still AM an otter, aren't I? Too bad about your discovery though. That's nice." He turned and continued to eat.

Michael's heart dropped. *He can read minds?*

"No, actually, although I WISH I could. At least in most circumstances, but not now. Not with you at least. You've been thinking aloud and it's bothering me. You know, people who talk a lot end up in jail."

What? "Now wait just a minute, Mr. Otter,"

"Chet's the name, but good try. Actually NOT."

"Like I was saying, Mr. Chet," Michael continued, angry again. After all, he would have to find another outlet for fame than animal discovery. "Who do you think you are coming in unexpectedly, eating all of my food, vanilla or not, and then being mean? Who does that?"

"Why, I do of course. What a silly question that was," Chet laughed. "I'm a king in these parts you know."

"Yeah right! If you're a king, why do you steal sub-par cookies from hungry children? What about that?"

"Well, they were available..."

"And another thing," Michael continued. "Do you know who I am? I mean, I'm not a king, but I certainly am more popular here than at my school." He was hoping that otters regarded him as highly as the other animals did.

"I know who you are," Chet snapped. "You're a rude little boy who can't keep his nose out of other people's business!"

"That's not my name!" Michael said indignantly.

"No, no it's not. It's much too long to be a proper name. I don't really care who you are."

"My name is Michael!"

"Yes, Mickey, whatever. Let me tell you. You've stumbled into the wrong cave. You see...I'm a villain. I'm just not that good!"

Chet looked into Michael's eyes and began to sing a terrible song about many terrible deeds. It was pretty catchy and Michael did his best not to clap along. After all, he didn't think it would help the situation. Probably smart. Michael occasionally has his flashes of brilliance. When Chet finished, he frowned and sighed.

"That wasn't one of my better performances, I'm a bit flat today. It must be the Vanilla Squares."

"You sing that a lot?" Michael asked, fascinated.

"Oh yes, yes for all sorts of animals, people and the like. I've even gotten an offer from Broadway you know."

Whatever Broadway was, Michael sincerely doubted that Chet would ever get there. He got up to leave.

"Oh? Leaving so soon?"

"I thought you didn't like me?"

"Oh don't get me wrong, Marco, I certainly don't, but wouldn't you like to stay just a bit longer?" Chet suddenly lit a match, revealing a pile of very human-like skeletons beneath them.

Michael gasped.

"I see you've noticed my collection. Good. That's why I lit this candle," Chet chuckled. "Intimidating isn't it? I would certainly love to add to it."

The otter's laughter filled the cavern as Michael scrambled out the entrance. He hit something hard and fell to the ground. It was Grohill.

"Who's that? Who's that?" the porcupine yelled, ready for a fight. "Why I should..."

"Grohill, it's me!" Michael said happily.

Doc stood beside him, still very much alive. (Thank goodness!) Well okay, chained up and extremely uncomfortable looking, but definitely alive. The same could not be said for the moss covered log Michael had rescued. Michael looked at his friends and laughed. They all laughed. Well, everyone except Chet.

"Not to break up the happy reunion or anything, but I'm still here," he said . "Now if any of you don't have any more food, I think I'll be on my way." He started to walk away, but turned, an evil smile on his face.

"Wait a second...Doc, is that you?" Chet said. "Oh, what a surprise we have here!"

Michael went over and stood beside the rabbit. Grohill watched, but kept his distance. Clearly, the time the two had spent together had not changed anything.

"You know this creature?" Michael asked pointing at Chet in surprise. "Why? How?"

"Now, Mitch, you know it's rude to point."

"And you would know a lot about rudeness, wouldn't you, Chet?" Doc said sternly. The otter looked taken aback, but said nothing. "Now, Michael, don't worry about him."

"Yeah, he's trouble!" Grohill said, then paused, realizing he'd agreed with Doc. "Can I take that back? I only sort of meant that. Sort of."

"Everyone around the village knows him." Doc said, shaking his head. "Why, he'll come around sometimes just to stir up trouble! Kind of like Lord Piper! A great many headaches he's caused me over the years."

"But Doc!" Michael said anxiously. "He has all sorts of skeletons in his cave and he..."

"Now, Michael, Chet may be trouble, but he's fairly harmless. We all have skeletons in our closet."

We do? I don't...do I? Hold the phone, that's wildly unexpected!!! Goodness, I need to check when I get home...Oh no....

"Sure he makes the fluff on the end of my tail stand on end, but this isn't even his cave!"

Chet frowned.

"But just because he's full of talk doesn't mean you shouldn't avoid him. Chet is one of Lord Piper's hooligans, Michael."

"Now wait just a minute, old-timer! I might be a hooligan, but I belong to no one. I do what I want!"

"Which is usually cause trouble," Grohill said.

"Hey, an otter's got to eat, right? It pays to be bad, Grover."

"You don't have to be bad though, Chet, you can do the right thing!" Michael said.

"Whatever, Mongo. If you want to know, I'm not working for Lord Piper at the moment. I'm working for a rather good-looking fellow named Dapply."

That's the same thing...

"He said to meet him at his hideout for payment. I was just on the way there when I ran into you. Thank you for the snacks by the way. Even though they were vanilla. So nasty..."

"Well you'll be unhappy to learn then that Dapply no longer has a hideout here. We were looking for him too. He's gone!" Grohill said triumphantly.

"Gone is he? And how do you know this, Groucho?" Chet said, suddenly angry.

"After we got separated, I knew we had to find Michael," Doc said. "I knew he would want to find us and that he'd probably try to meet up at Dapply's hideout. Grohill finally gave in and let me tell him where the pyrcantheon grew. We.."

"When we got there," Grohill interrupted. "We found that his hideout was deserted. It didn't look like anyone had been there for quite some time. The pyrcantheon was destroyed."

"You're just saying that," Chet said, a look of disgust on his face. "You don't know how hard I've worked. How much I've been through. Do you know what it's like to be me? Do you? To be disrespected because of who I am? Just because I'm in a line of work people don't understand? Chet the Devious, they call me. Chet the Discouraging. Do you know what it's like to have grown up with these names?"

No, but if he had said 'Chet the Large'...

"Now Chet, you and I both know you came from a loving family," Doc said with concern. "Why, I had

Engwald and Elmira over for tea just the day before Tuesday. Those names are a product of your own actions, your choices. You know you can always come home."

"Oh stop it, Donald! Let's not play pretend now. There's enough hijinks going on in this forest as it is. Stop joshing me!" Chet said. "My parents don't love me! They just want to use my good looks like that Dapply fellow. Maybe make a quick buck on Broadway with my singing."

Singing, again?

"I thought Dapply would understand, but apparently I was wrong. Why I have half a mind to track him down and teach him what otters are REALLY about."

Swimming?

Not having talked in a while, which was rare, Michael sat to the side processing everything he'd heard. He didn't trust this Chet character. If he was working with Dapply, then he was working with Lord Piper.

And if Dapply isn't where we think he is, but couldn't be where he isn't, he must be where we don't think he is! Where IS he?

"We're not sure, Michael," Doc said.

Dern fern! Thinking aloud again.

"Do we know of any other pyrcantheon? Maybe he has a different hideout or something," Michael reasoned.

"Now why do you lunkheads keep talking about flowers?" Chet said. "I'm trying to find the man who stole my money."

"And so are we," Michael said. "Well, more or less. He doesn't have any of my money,"

"You're eleven!"

"But..."

"Get to the point!"

"Right. Umm..." Michael said, flustered. "We met a mouse who told us he saw a deep purple flower on the well dressed man who attacked him. We think that the flower was pyrcantheon and that the man was Dapply."

"Yes, yes, Max, I'm not that stupid go on."

Michael continued. "So we figured that Dapply's hideout must be somewhere near these flowers in order for him to wear a fresh one every day and...wait a second. I know where there are more flowers!"

195

"Outside. Tell me something I don't know, Michael."

"My school!" Michael yelled excitedly. Doc clapped his paws in triumph. Grohill smiled uneasily, but said nothing.

Michael paused. "Wait a second...Did you just call me Michael?"

Chet looked taken aback. "I certainly did not call you that, Molly. And if I did, it was certainly by accident. Don't let it go to your head or anything. Seriously, what's wrong with you?"

Michael sighed. "Whatever. Something has been bothering me this whole time and that's what it is! The same deep purple flower, a pyrcantheon, or whatever you call it, grows right outside my classroom window! I see it every day when I stay inside during recess to learn more."

"Michael, that's great news!" Doc said.

"So, where is this school then? We better get going," Chet said. "Not that I want to hang out at an institution of learning, rather boring if you ask me."

"What do you mean 'we'?" Michael asked.

"If you think I'm going to let that dandy play me the fool you're wrong. I'm coming."

Aghast, Michael looked around at his companions. Grohill looked horrified, but Doc shrugged. Michael didn't like Chet the Discouraging Otter, but what choice did they have? If Chet WAS working for Lord Piper, then keeping him in their sight was the best thing they could do. Then he would have no way of reporting where they were, right?

"Fine. But as soon as we find Dapply, you're gone."

"I wasn't asking. And I wouldn't stick around a second longer. Hanging out with you three isn't exactly my idea of a good time."

Michael wasn't sure what Chet's idea of a good time was, but he didn't want to know. It might be something like super scary.

The four companions, or whatever you want to call them, took off toward Some Town Primary School at a brisk pace. *Yes! School!* Michael thought excitedly.

197

"I thought otters were supposed to be happy and nice?" Michael said angrily. "At least that's what Tommy Snaggletooth told me. You're not happy, you're just mean and discouraging! Why can't you be more like the happy otter at the zoo that had a cell phone?"

"I am happy, Montgomery," the otter said, a sinister smile creeping across his face. "Really, happy."

"Whatever."

Chet had been encouraging Grohill to abuse Doc the whole time and it was making Michael sick. He didn't know what he could do though, he needed them on his side. He needed EVERYBODY on his side.

Is this what it means to be a hero? he wondered. *Letting people get hurt so you can protect the greater good? I'm not sure I want to be a hero if that's the case.*

(Sneaky Pete makes it look SO easy...)

When they got to school it was almost nightfall. Everyone had left for the day, even Grumpy Old Ms. Jones.

She's usually the last to leave because she stays behind eating the souls of children she made cry during the day, Michael thought, surprised at her absence.

Evidently, their rendezvous on Charley's Knob hadn't made much of an impression on him. *My wounds from her are too deep to heal,* he sighed, looking around. As for her sister....*Now where's Dapply?*

"I don't think he's here anymore," Doc said.

"Then we wait," Grohill said definitively.

Chet nodded and walked deeper into the woods. The rest of the animals followed him. They made Michael search the grounds alone while they waited by the fire. It was a chilly night and no one had offered to help except for Chet. Michael declined. It left him in a no good, rotten mood.

Like one-month-old pudding rotten.

He was increasingly curious about the frog's book, but hadn't had another chance to look at it. He'd been so distracted with everything that had been going on!

- CHAPTER 24 -

What is my role in all of this? he wondered. *I'm starting to think the problems of animals are better left to veterinarians. I'm not even considering that as a career choice.*

The other animals fell asleep by the fire while he kept watch.

They look so peaceful, he thought. *Even Chet who's a jerk, which is kind of surprising. Grohill too, actually. But they also look so asleep too, so I guess now's my chance!*

Quickly and quietly he crept away into the darkness, stepping lightly so as not to wake the others. He knew he shouldn't leave his watch, but he knew just the perfect spot to look at the book. Earlier in the day, they'd stopped for water at a large pond about a half mile away. That wasn't too far for him to walk even though he was slow and generally out of shape.

No one will find me there, he thought. *AND I can wash down my Vanilla Squares while I read. Yuck*

But as he got closer to the pond, he heard two voices. Change of plans. And from the sound of it, they were arguing. (Not cool!)

"I don't know why you always bring this up, Phil. We're related. I can't date you."

"Oh, Jennifer, you're just saying that because you don't like me and you don't want to hurt my feelings. Well I've got news for you. I'm a man, I can handle it."

"That would be the day."

"Seriously, Jennifer? Seriously?"

"Phil, we both have the same last name. I'm an octo-pus, and you're a platy-pus. We're practically brother and sister."

"Jennifer, I've known you my whole life. We don't look anything alike!"

"Phil, I'm not going to talk about this right now."

"After everything we've been through? Surely you think we need each other? These are dark times after all."

"Ah now don't go bringing that up again, Phil! You know Lord Piper isn't after us. He's after that boy Michael Pumpkin, or whatever his name is."

Dern fern. Michael urgently took out the compass, but the dial had disappeared. He sighed with relief. Leaning in closer, he hoped to learn something he could share with the others. His heart was racing fast, but it was apparently no time to panic. Yet.

"You know, Jen," the platypus started.

"Don't call me Jen, I hate that," the octopus said.

"Like I was saying, Jennifer, sweetheart, I feel kind of sorry for the boy. I mean, what's he done anyway to deserve all this mess?"

"What's he done?!" Jennifer laughed. "He hasn't done anything yet, that's the point. You know the legend. A boy comes from the outside world to defeat Lord Piper. It's been passed down for generations. Probably even before there WAS a Lord Piper. He's not stupid. He thinks this Michael kid might be that boy. He's evaded Piper's grasp already, crafty kid. That's why Lord Piper has Dapply and the others looking for him."

The others? Michael gasped. *I'm glad I'm popular, but like, okay. Dapply...the rats...Chet, perhaps...and?*

(...and the others! Good job, Michael!)

"I heard this Michael kid's not alone though, that he's got a big army," Phil said.

"Oh that's what they say. Chet told me he only has an irritable porcupine and an old rabbit with him. Some army that is. And get this. The porcupine beats the rabbit every night when the boy isn't looking! Ha!" Jennifer laughed again. Her high-pitched voice was beginning to irritate Michael. Well that, and what she was saying.

"Lord Piper only wants the boy though. He's given orders to kill the others. They're probably closing in on them right now."

Oh gosh, I hope not!

Michael had heard enough. He looked down at the compass and the arrow was going crazy. Worst of all, it was pointing directly at their camp! Quickly grabbing his things he took off at a full sprint. Gasping for air, he cursed Chet under his breath.

"That traitor! When did he tell them? What did he tell them?"

Michael was so furious, he promised himself he would skin the otter alive if he had the chance. The camp site was probably still half a mile away. He hadn't gotten anywhere...he wasn't very fast. He'd never make it! Then suddenly, he stopped.

- CHAPTER 24 -

If I just come crashing in there, they'll get me too.

He walked the last half-mile slowly and deliberately so as not to attract any undue attention to himself. Good idea, but again, it was slow. Anything could have happened. He was feeling pretty good about his sneaking abilities when all of a sudden a voice behind him spoke.

"Just where do you think YOU'RE going?"

Michael's heart skipped a beat.

Oh good, it's Doc, he thought, relieved. *But why did he have to use such a threatening phrase?*

"You okay, son? I woke up and didn't find you by the fire. I was worried you might be out freezing to death."

A look of deep concern spread across the old rabbit's face as he held up a blanket. Michael took it and thanked him. Something was bothering him.

"But Doc, how did you get away? You guys were being attacked! The compass! I..." All of the emotions from the last few days were pouring out. He couldn't help it.

"Well if we were under attack that's news to me," Doc said, taking the compass from Michael. The dial had stopped spinning. "The only one of us who might wake up with a headache is Grohill and I don't think he'll remember anything. I hit him pretty good."

205

"You hit Grohill?" Michael said, surprised.

"Well sure, I had to! How else would I get away?" Doc laughed. "You see, Michael, I could have slipped Grohill's rope any time. I just wanted to create the illusion that he was in control. I wanted to find out what he's up to and that was the only way."

"But he beats you every night!" Michael said. "You let him do that? Why? I can't believe I didn't stop him. You must think I'm the worst person you've ever met."

Doc smiled. "Now, Michael, you know you're not! I have quite a positive impression of you," he chuckled.

"You just think I'm awesome because of some legend or something. I'm not that guy!"

"You're not yet, Michael, but you WILL be. And you protect me in the little ways. I thank you for that. Your day will come when you need to stand up to Grohill. The hardest task any man can face is to stand up to a friend. Your time will come."

"But Doc, I don't know who to believe!"

"It's not important right now who you believe, Michael, for I fear that Grohill knows more than he's telling us. It's important that you believe in yourself. Can you do that for me?"

"But Doc, Chet, he..."

"You mean how he's been communicating where we are to Lord Piper? Michael, Chet isn't the type of animal to fight. Sure, he might act tough, but he's as scared as anyone I've ever seen. He means to use us as ransom in exchange for his own life. When you found him in the woods he wasn't looking for Dapply, he was running away from him!"

If Doc found any of this information surprising, he certainly didn't betray it lightly. Michael wiped the tears from his eyes.

"Do you think he means to carry it out then? To turn us in, I mean? I just heard two animals talking by the pond. They said Lord Piper is after us, and he's not the only one! Doc, what can we do? We're running out of time! I'm not ready!"

"We just have to keep doing what we're doing, Michael. I've found over the years that the best place to keep my enemies is close by. Not that I've had that many, mind you," he chuckled, "but I've learned a lesson or two from Lord Piper himself, believe it or not! You see, he wouldn't come around the village just to mock us. He wanted to know what we were up to, if we were planning an attack. And I guess our indifference made him furious."

"But how can we fight him? We don't have any weapons! I don't even know what we're going to do when we find Dapply! I don't know martial arts. I don't have throwing stars. I don't have a cape or secret mask...I..."

"We'll use what we have, Michael. Like that old book you've been looking at for starters."

The book! Michael gasped. *He didn't see it, did he? This guy knows EVERYTHING.* Quickly, Michael tried to shove it into his fanny pack. This amused the old rabbit.

"Now son, there's no use hiding it now. That's about the seventeenth time I've seen it!" he laughed. "You're always trying to look at it when you think I'm asleep. Rest is hard to come by for someone my age. Goodness knows I need it. Now I know you don't trust me. But if there's anything in that book I need to know, please tell me."

"But that's just it!" Michael said. "I haven't opened it! I've been trying to, but I haven't been able to get away. I was trying to look at it now when I ran into Phil and Jen..."

"Phil and Jen?"

"The platypus and octopus. Phil loves Jennifer, but she doesn't feel the same way."

"What?"

"Oh never mind, that's not important."

"Not right now, I certainly wouldn't think so," Doc laughed.

Michael was getting tired of waiting to see what the mysterious frog had given him. It was worse than the week before Christmas! What did it matter if Doc saw what was in it? He knew about the book so there was nothing to lose. Plus, if he had to go with his hunch then he thought he could trust the rabbit.

"It's now or never," he said opening it up. He didn't know what he'd expected to find. A blinding light. Maybe a different language. But the pages were mostly blank, a few stained or hardened on the edges from age. (Kind of a letdown if you ask me)

They sat together in stunned silence and Michael's mind wandered to the other animals. To Schumer. To poor old Cephas and Mama Mable. To Sneaks and the club.

I thought I could save them. Now I just know I was being stupid, he thought, sadly. *At least no one will miss me at school. I'll be dead soon.* He thought of his family and what they would be doing right now. *Dad's probably going to work. I don't know how he gets up before the sun. It must be hard to find his office! Mom's probably trying to go back to sleep after Dad woke her up on his way out. But she'll get up soon and eat breakfast in her purple bathrobe. Then she'll do the crossword before Ralph wakes up. Life goes on, I guess. Call the search party off!*

"At least we can eat the empty pages if we get hungry," Michael sighed.

He began contemplating who he would want to speak at his funeral. Ralph? No way. Oliver? Maybe, but he's hard to get in touch with. Miss Dandelion? Definitely.

"Michael, look at this!" Doc said suddenly.

A message had appeared on the page. The red ink of the flowing script looked like blood. It was frightening.

(How ominous...)

"I recognize this handwriting," Doc said.

"You do?"

"Oh yes, but I can't place where. I think it's from some of our most ancient writings about the founding of the village. Michael, this must be important!"

They bent down eagerly and read together.

A wise man does not waste what he has been given. Rather, he takes it and turns it into something more. This requires patience and understanding.

Recall the winemaker who sold all of his finest wine to the king's men, but kept nothing for the king himself! All that he was left with was the lees! But what could the master winemaker do when the king came to collect his wine? He had nothing to give him! The winemaker, unable to satisfy the king, was thrown in jail.

Years later when he died, lonely and without a family, the king sent his men to reclaim the man's home. Upon their arrival, they could hardly believe themselves when they found that the winemaker had left them one last parting gift. Taking what remained of the wine from years ago, they brought it to the king who declared it the sweetest wine he'd ever tasted.

"I was wrong to imprison this winemaker so hastily," he said. "For the lees have sweetened it beyond any that I have ever tasted. Surely this speaks to the longevity of my kingdom and the need for patience in my rule!"

And from that day forth, the old king never laid a hand on another soul, instead seeking peace in the land. Unfortunately for him, his kingdom met an untimely, bloody and disgusting demise, but that wasn't until after his time.

So the tale was right in a way. Just wrong too.

"That's it!?!" Michael said angrily, wishing the pages had just stayed blank. "That's worse than nothing, what does that even mean?" He looked over at Doc, but the rabbit appeared to be just as confused as he was. "This was our last hope!"

All of the energy drained out of him. He regretted not having a cleaner favorite shirt to wear at his burial.

"Curious, very, very curious," Doc said, ignoring Michael. He was still staring at the book. Michael couldn't imagine what the rabbit was looking at. The book was worthless! In fact, he planned on donating it to the school library the very next morning.

They give you half-off of lunch-room pizza for every book you donate! he thought, excitedly. *I'm starving!*

But Doc continued to stare at the page. After a moment he paused, gathering his words carefully.

"I understand your disappointment Michael, I really do. I haven't the foggiest what this means either! But we shouldn't second guess it. Why would the frog have given it to you otherwise?"

"Because he thought I was some sort of hero," Michael snapped. "Well he's wrong!" (No I wasn't)

"I'm not a hero! I'm just some fat kid who took the wrong way to school. The only thing this book is good for is keeping the fire going!"

Doc scowled. "Don't doubt fate, Michael, I've heard this story before, I just can't place where. Not too many people know it, I don't think. That makes it extremely important. It's undoubtedly a clue!"

"Yeah right. Whatever you say, Doc. I'm sure it's REALLY important..."

"It HAS to do with defeating Lord Piper, Michael it just HAS to. That's the only thing that would make sense. I would die to protect this information."

"Then you would die in vain!"

Doc scowled and continued to think aloud about any possible explanations.

Only half-listening, Michael pretended to start a fire with the book, warming his hands over the pages. He smiled at the rabbit, but Doc didn't smile back.

"Can you not focus for a minute?" Doc said angrily. "If you would stop feeling sorry for yourself maybe you would realize that we don't need a fire, it's morning."

Michael looked up and saw that the sun was shining through the trees. He realized he wasn't cold anymore and stuffed the blanket into the fanny pack.

This thing is endless, he thought. *But how did it get to be morning? We must have fallen asleep at some point, I guess. Either that, or last night was shorter than usual.*

He was going to ask Doc about it when he realized the rabbit was avoiding eye contact with him. Suddenly, he felt very, very small.

"Doc, I'm sorry," he said as they walked back to the campsite. "It's just that...I've never been on an adventure before, and I'm not sure what to do. I thought it would be easy. But I'm hungry and I'm scared. I haven't slept well in nights! There's a man in a suit after me. And a fox. And a guy with a gun. Sneaky Pete makes it look so easy..."

"Michael, Sneaky Pete isn't real. He's just a comic book character," Doc snapped. "Real life isn't that easy! It's not supposed to be easy!"

Sneaky Pete isn't real?

While this moment was truly earth shattering for Michael, he tried to hide it. Admitting his mistake certainly wouldn't make it any easier.

"I don't care that it's hard," Michael said. "That's not it. I mean, I do care because things that are hard are you know, hard. It's just that this doesn't seem like my life! Me, Michael Pumpernickel. I'm talking to a rabbit!"

"And I'm talking to a human!" Doc said smiling, trying to hide his amusement. The anger between them had subsided. "You can imagine my surprise the first time I saw you. I never thought I would see the day when another human would enter Burlwood Forest."

"Another human?" Michael asked. What did Doc mean by that?!?!

But Doc never had a chance to answer him. They had arrived back at the campsite and Grohill was up, pacing back and forth and muttering loudly to himself.

"There you are!" he said glaring at Doc. "Put your noose back on, old man. We've wasted so much time. We might have missed Dapply! Yes! We might have missed him! Michael, why didn't you tell me it was daytime?" he scolded. "Chet, get up you good-for-nothing, lazy..."

"Watch it!" the otter yelled as Grohill hit him on the head. "For your information, we haven't missed him. He should be arriving in about 10 seconds."

"What?" Michael asked.

"9."

"Look if this is some sort of game then just stop. We outnumber you."

"8."

"Chet, I said stop, really!"

"6...Oh wait, 7."

"I'm not even speaking to you," the porcupine decided, turning his back to the otter.

""You might want to get out there," Chet said, motioning to the patch of grass between the woods and the carpool lane. "He'll be here any second."

"That's ridiculous," Grohill said. "How would YOU know where Dapply was?" Michael looked at Doc. Both of them knew *exactly* why Chet knew where Dapply was.

"...and 1....now! Quick!" Chet yelled suddenly.

"Ahh where? Where?" Grohill said running into the street. A van narrowly missed him, screeching to a stop in front of the school. Darting back and forth, the porcupine danced around trying to avoid the oncoming wave of cars.

Morning carpool, Michael chuckled.

The memories of simpler times couldn't help but bring a smile to his face. *I should be there*, he thought. *I wonder who they replaced me with on the safety patrol? Certainly not someone of my caliber?*

Concerned about the prestige of his former post and slightly worried about Grohill's safety, he ventured out into the road behind him.

"Michael, no!" Doc yelled, but he was too late. Michael was already out of reach.

It wasn't the string of cars that worried Doc. Michael had looked both ways so he was safe. It wasn't even Grohill's erratic behavior that made him nervous, although he DID cause a few fender benders.

It was the fact that the driver of the van was visibly angry and standing outside of his car, yelling at the person behind him. Which wouldn't have been a big deal if he hadn't been just the man they were looking for.

You got it. Dapply.

Oh, heavens to Betsy!

When Michael recognized him, it was too late. He tried to change direction, but his legs wouldn't let him. He sprinted across the carpool lane and ran headfirst into the van by accident.

"Michael?" a voice said.

A large boy, roughly double Michael's height and weight stood in front of him blocking the sun. Michael blinked, but his vision was still too blurry from the collision. He would just have to guess who it was.

"Mom?" he asked.

But it wasn't his mom. It was Jasper 'Big Boy' Clemmons. And Jasper let him know who he was with a right hook to the side of the head. Michael staggered backwards. *My mom would never do that...*

Hearing the commotion, Dapply released the other driver from a headlock and came over.

"Jasper! You know it's rude to hit strangers. Who is this boy?" Dapply asked, irritated at the interruption of his altercation.

"He hit your car, Dad. He's just some kid from my class."

"Is he?" Dapply said, recognizing Michael. "Are you close to this boy, Jasper?"

Sensing trouble, Michael tried to back away, but found that he couldn't. Dapply had him pinned. *He's Jasper's dad? Well that explains a lot. Actually, that gives me a lot more questions.*

Looking around for help, he saw that Grohill had run back into the forest. *Coward. It's not cool when you finally find the guy you're looking for and you decide you don't want to see him...*

"Oh, I hit him a few times a day probably," Jasper laughed. "My fist and his face are pretty close."

"Can you keep a secret, son?" Dapply asked, glancing around.

"Sure Dad! But I already know you cry when you watch romantic comedies and touching car commercials."

"No son, not that!" Dapply snapped. "I don't want you to tell anyone about that! But you can't tell them about what I'm about to do either."

Jasper stared at him blankly. "Well sure, Dad, I know you have your book club on Thursday mornings."

"Not that, son!"

"You mean you're going to try on that hula skirt I saw you buy at Super Duper Save yesterday? What you do in your own private time is none of my business no matter how strange it is."

Dapply grabbed Michael and shoved him into the back of his van. Surprised, Jasper jumped, knocking the door back open. Grumpy Old Ms. Jones, who was talking to a parent a few cars down, turned and walked towards them.

Wow, I never thought I would be glad to see her, Michael thought.

"Mr. Clemmons, what are you doing?" she asked, a concerned look on her face. "Why is Michael in the back of your van?"

"Umm..."

"Wait a second, Michael! Where HAVE you been?" she said. "We've been worried sick!" She didn't mention anything about their meeting on Charley's Knob.

Right. I bet you haven't noticed I've been gone.

"And you've already missed a test!"

Oh no, a test?! I've waited all summer for that! Michael thought, horrified. But his disgust wasn't as great as Dapply's. The organist didn't look like he was feeling well at the moment.

"Hello, Margaret," Dapply said regaining his composure and clamping his hand over Jasper's mouth. "My son and I were just showing Michael here...is that what you said his name was? We were showing him our new van. So much space. Isn't that right, boys?"

"Yes, so much space," Michael said nervously. Jasper's response was a little harder to understand.

"Mr. Clemmons, why are you covering Jasper's mouth? It looks like he wants to say something!" Grumpy Old Ms. Jones said, confused.

"I...ummm...he..." Dapply said, finally removing his hand.

"Dad, this van isn't new. We've had it for years!"

"Quiet, Jasper. I'll deal with you later," Dapply snapped. He raised his hand and shot his son a glance that could kill. He probably wanted it to. "Yes, Margaret. What I meant to say is that Mario and Jasper here were just planning a sleepover for tonight. I overheard them and said hey, why can't you have it here in the van? They were SO excited they just couldn't wait!"

Man, he's good, Michael thought.

(Not really, but...)

Jasper looked at Dapply, very much confused. Sensing his son was about to give them away again, Dapply continued.

"But, Margaret, I'm guessing that you're not here to talk about sleepovers. You know I'm a married man. You must want Jasper here for safety patrol! He's so excited about his new position, aren't you, Jasper?" he said pinching his son's cheeks.

No!

"Why he just couldn't stop talking about it on the way over!" Dapply said, his smile so fake it made Michael sick. Grumpy Old Ms. Jones on the other hand, fell for it completely. Jasper rolled his eyes and shot Michael a dangerous glance.

"If you don't want to do safety patrol, I'll do it," Michael mouthed him.

Japser considered it for a moment, but sneered. "You're right, father! Why, I just can't wait. Oh Ms. Jones, when do I start? Golly gee, this is just the best day of my life!"

That's probably the most polite thing he's ever said, Michael thought, angry and astonished at the same time. And he said it just to bother me! Michael felt honored. *Still, I'm surprised he could put that sentence together. He's made some real progress! Wow! Too bad everything he just said is a lie, though.*

Michael looked at Ms. Jones, eager not to be left alone with Dapply. To his relief, the bell rang indicating the start of the school day.

"Oh my, the mornings just fly by, don't they?" she said. "Well, Mr. Clemmons, I'll be taking Jasper to class now instead. He'll have to start safety patrol tomorrow. Come along now, children."

Dapply shot Michael a menacing look as they walked towards the school building. He'd missed his chance and he knew it. They both had. But Michael was too relieved to worry about it. He was excited about school!

Dapply went to get in his van, but reconsidered. "You won't get away next time!" he yelled shaking his fist in Michael's direction.

The car behind him started to honk. It looked like the man from the chokehold was starting to get some courage after all. Bold!

"What did you say, Mr. Clemmons?" Ms. Jones asked, pausing on the sidewalk, a confused look on her face.

"I said...ummm...Have a good day next time!" Dapply yelled and sped away.

"I'm glad that guy's gone," Michael said aloud by mistake.

"That guy's my dad!" Jasper said.

Grumpy Old Ms. Jones stepped in between them and ushered them into the building. Before he entered, Michael caught a glimpse of Doc staring at him from the woods. He looked worried. That made Michael feel kind of bad...

Of course, Michael thought. *In all the excitement, I blew it. I have to rejoin the others.*

"Umm....Ms. Jones?" Michael said.

"Yes, Michael, what is it?"

"I umm...left my backpack at home...I think."

Man, this thinking on the spot is hard business. I'll never get a spot on an improvisational comedy troupe now!

"It's okay, Michael, you can just borrow a pen and some paper from Jasper. Then when you go home tonight you..." She paused, then jumped as if she suddenly remembered something. "Home! Of course! Home! Michael, where have you been? Your family has been worried sick about you. Why, they sent out a search party just last night."

Last night? Haven't I been gone for a week? he wondered, shaking his head. *And hasn't that search party guy been after me the whole time? Who IS that guy? I'm not sure I actually have any idea what is going on. Figures, I'd screw up my FIRST adventure...*

"They even had dogs I think," she said. "But now that you're here of course, there's no need for a search party. I'll call your mother right away."

EVEN WORSE THAN DOGS! he gasped.

Despite the fact that his family had *apparently* just noticed his absence, he figured he would be in a lot of trouble. He'd never run away, or been gone for an extended period of time before. He'd never even missed a meal! Of course, he'd missed quite a few over the last few days.

I must be skin and bones, he thought.

But he couldn't figure out who the other search party was if it wasn't the one that his parents had sent. His heart began to beat quickly.

"Here we go, Michael," Ms. Jones said smiling. "You and Jasper can sit here in the office while I call your mother. It'll be just a second. Oh, and I'm glad you're safe," she added. "Miss Dandelion will be SO pleased! She's been really worried about you."

Miss Dandelion, Michael sighed.

If he needed any motivation to complete his quest, she was it. *I know she thinks she's too old for me, but I'll never give up! We were made for each other. I'll NEVER love anyone else!*

And then everything changed.

They hadn't been in Principal Goodburn's office for more than a minute when the most beautiful girl Michael had ever seen walked in. So much for Miss Dandelion, right?

The girl looked around nervously, like she wasn't sure she was in the right place, taking in her surroundings with a confused expression on her face. Michael gasped as she walked towards him, her long brown hair sparkling in the light.

"Umm...excuse me," she asked, uncertainly. "Is this the principal's office?"

Michael stared at her blankly, his mouth hanging open. The girl smiled as she set her backpack down and took out some papers.

"I'm new here, I just wanted to give him my transcript."

Michael blinked and tried to form a sentence. "Umm...yeah this is it! He's not here right now though. My name is Michael!" His voice squeaked with excitement. Jasper laughed.

The girl looked at the bully disapprovingly and continued. "Hi Michael, it's nice to meet you!" she said, brightly. "The teachers call me Elizabeth, but my REAL name is Crispin. Crispin Elizabeth Rye. That's what my transcript says, see?" She held it out in front of him. Jasper leaned in to get a better look, but she pulled it away.

"Anyway," she continued, scoffing at the bully. "I just wanted to find out where my class was. I got mail that said I'm in Margaret Jones' class. Do you know Ms. Jones, Michael?"

Do I? Michael thought excitedly. *That means we're in the same class!* Suddenly, he forgot all about Lord Piper and his imminent death.

"Of course," he said. "I'M in her class too!"

"That's great!" Crispin said, her eyes lighting up. "Maybe we can be best friends!"

Or more... Michael thought happily.

"I'm from out of town so I didn't think I would make any friends the first day."

229

- CHAPTER 26 -

"I'll be your friend," Jasper said anxiously.

Crispin glared at him. "We'll see," she said. "Anyway, I should probably get to class. It was nice meeting you, Michael."

"It was nice meeting you too, Crispin!" Michael said. "I love you," he added softly so no one could hear him.

But apparently Crispin HAD heard him. She smiled as she gathered her things and left the office. Jasper grunted and slammed his fist against the wall. It shook the whole room, but wasn't enough to bring Michael out of his daze.

I've never seen someone so beautiful, he thought. *Her face will be in my mind forever. The freckles...her smile. I'll never forget the way she looked at me.*

"What's that you have there, dweeb?" Jasper said, snatching something out of Michael's hands. Evidently, he was still mad about Crispin's rejection.

What? Michael wondered.

He'd been too busy trying to make sense of his feelings for Crispin that he didn't remember taking anything out of his fanny pack. He felt so conflicted. Even though Miss Dandelion was a lot older than him and Crispin was his age, he felt guilty, like he had betrayed her in some way.

What did Jasper just take? he wondered. Suddenly, he panicked. *Oh no, the book!*

Of course, he didn't know why it was important, but he had a feeling that if it got in the wrong hands, they were all dead. *Jaspers hands were definitely wrong!*

"Let it go, that's mine!" he said defiantly, grabbing the book in Jasper's hands.

"No it's not. It's Principal Goodburn's," Jasper said pushing him aside.

Michael looked down and saw that they were holding a copy of 'Wild Animal in the Wild: A Biography of a Wild Animal.' *What? How did I get that?* Jasper snatched it from him and he sat back.

He looked around, seeing the room for the first time.

Principal Goodburn is such a weirdo, Michael thought. *This place gives me the creeps*. He was surrounded by cages filled with the strangest animals you could think of. Fish, birds, cats, dogs, they were all there! Well, it wasn't the animals that were weird. They were all common household pets. No, it was the quantity that concerned Michael.

I think they're all watching me, he thought, curling into a ball onto the floor. *Not even my favorite shirt could protect me from THIS!*

He took out the compass to see which one was the most dangerous, but it was blank. *Drat!*

Sensing his fear, the dogs began to growl loudly. The cats hissed back at them and the birds screeched just for fun. *This is bananas!* The fish even began to do some sort of strange dance that Michael was sure had some sort of dark purpose to it.

"They ARE pretty scary, I have to agree with you on that," Jasper said in a surprising display of decency. He sat down on the floor next to Michael. "Which one is your least favorite?"

"That one!" Michael said pointing to a large black lab in the far corner. "Every time I come in here...so this time and the one other time I did, she stares at me. It's like...she wants to eat me or something!"

"Now Mr. Pumpernickel, you know Suzie would never hurt you!" Principal Goodburn chuckled coming into the room. "She likes the older kids, like Mr. Clemmons here." Jasper whimpered and started to crawl towards the door. (Can't blame him for that)

"Oh now don't be scared, Mr. Clemmons, I was only joking. You'd think you would know that by now. After all, we've gotten to know each other quite well these past ten years, haven't we?"

What? I'm barely eleven!

Principal Goodburn smiled, walking over and patting Jasper on the head. Irritated, the bully pushed his hand aside, knocking it into the side of a large cage next to him. The effect was instantaneous. Whatever was in the cage started to screech loudest of all!

"Look what you've done now, Mr. Clemmons," Principal Goodburn said disapprovingly. "You've disturbed my ferrets!" Opening the cage, he got out the ugliest one and began to stroke its fur lovingly. It jumped up and bit his face, causing it to bleed.

"Cute animals, aren't they?" he said as the blood flowed down his cheek. "All of them I mean. Aren't they wonderful? I just love animals!" Principal Goodburn began to sing.

What is WITH people around here? Michael wondered. *I'm beginning to reassess my position on singing in everyday life.*

But he didn't have time to dwell on it. He'd have to think about it later. Mercifully, Ms. Jones returned from the back room, interrupting his thoughts. Although truthfully, Principal Goodburn wasn't *that* bad a tenor.

"Your mother is not very happy Michael, but after I assured her that you're safe and sound, she stopped screeching. At least...I thought that was her. What's going on in here? Are you singing, Lionel?"

"Why, hahaha...Margaret! Why would you ever ask such a thing?" Principal Goodburn said, blushing. "Don't be preposterous! Seriously, me???? How, silly. It was Mr. Clemmons!"

"Was it really you, Jasper?"

"NO! Are you kidding me? I don't sing! Why would I do that?!?!"

"I was just about to say, it was really good..."

"Then it WAS me!" Jasper and Principal Goodburn said together.

"Umm..."

"Hahaha...haha..ummm..." Principal Goodburn said uneasily. "Mr. Pumpernickel, Mr. Clemmons and I were just admiring my ferret, Blinky, here. Say hello to Ms. Jones, Blinky!" The ferret screeched. "You know, Margaret, I think this one here has quite an affinity for animals," he said pointing at Jasper. "Why, look what he's reading! Wild Animals in the Wild was one of my favorites at his age. Look at me now!"

Jasper looked very, very sick.

Yeah, I wouldn't want to turn into that guy either, Michael thought. *Although I doubt Jasper can read anyway. I want to be like Sneaky Pete, not him! A hero.*

That made him think about the others.

Wait!

Maybe some of the animals in the room could help him! Scooting over towards a cage with an overweight cat in it, he began to motion to get its attention. The cat turned away. What did he expect?

LET'S GET ONE THING STRAIGHT...CATS
DON'T LIKE YOU. THEY LIKE THEMSELVES.

Michael motioned to a bird in the far corner, but it
didn't say anything either. Instead, it was bobbing its head
to the music of its own heart.

What's wrong with these animals? Michael thought.
Why won't they talk to me?

He was really discouraged. And then it hit him.
Schumer had been right all along!

"The trees ARE magic!"

"What?" Grumpy Old Ms. Jones asked.

"I believe what Mr. Pumpernickel means, Margaret,
is that he's developing an affinity for the outdoors too. He's
discovered what a wonderful place it is." Principal
Goodburn began to sing again, but stopped himself.

Michael turned red. *I can't believe no animal
stepped foot outside of the forest before! I mean...this was
pretty easy to figure out once I did. The trees are magic! An
animal who knows this could be really powerful. I guess he
could either share it with everyone else, or maybe just use
it for evil. Wonderful,* Michael thought.

The only one who believed in the magic trees was Lord Piper and his followers. *That's not good.*

As Principal Goodburn began to give Ms. Jones and Jasper a thrilling account of the third chapter of 'Wild Animals,' Michael glanced out the window trying to figure out what Lord Piper would do with that information. He just couldn't wrap his head around it.

It's important, but...what? he wondered. The implications were huge, regardless.

The window was partially blocked by a tower of cages, but Michael could see Chet and Grohill standing by the flagpole.

Thank goodness, they're okay! he sighed, relieved. They weren't alone though. They appeared to be laughing at something in front of them.

That's not fair, what are they doing? he thought. *They should be looking for Dapply. Or Doc! This isn't the time for fun and games. We have to save the forest!* But then he saw something that made his heart skip a beat.

It wasn't a flag tied to the pole.

It WAS Doc.

Instantly, Michael was overwhelmed with anger. Even though he and Doc hadn't left on the best terms, the rabbit had been about to tell him something important. He was a good guy!

"I've got to get out of here RIGHT NOW!" Michael yelled, suddenly darting for the door.

Taken aback, Principal Goodburn jumped in front of him to block the way, dropping the ferret onto the ground.

"Blinky! Blinky!" he yelled, changing his mind and chasing after the animal.

Unable to think of anything else to do but scream, Jasper began wailing at the top of his lungs, running around the room to avoid the ferret.

It was complete pandemonium! Dogs barking, birds screeching. It's no wonder the entire school didn't stop by to see what in the world was going on! But since most of the administration was used to Principal Goodburn's queer habits, no one did. I guess they were learning?

Grumpy Old Ms. Jones took a deep breath. "Thursdays," she sighed.

"QUIETTTTTTTTTTTTTTTTTTTTTTTTTTT!!!!!" she yelled, her face turning purple from the effort.

The room became silent.

"That's better," she said.

Maybe this isn't such a good time to leave, Michael thought, *but do I really have a choice? Doc is in trouble!* He rocked back in forth, wrestling with his indecision. *Hey, wait. What the heck is up with Jasper?* he wondered.

The bully was grimacing and dancing around in place.

He's not half bad at that, actually, Michael thought. *Maybe I've pegged him the wrong way all along?*

Shaking his head as if coming out of some sort of trance, Principal Goodburn looked at Jasper and smiled.

"It looks like Mr. Clemmons has found Blinky!"

Ohhhhh...

"Are you okay? I'm so sorry!" Goodburn said soothingly, grabbing the ferret.

"I'm...I'm fine," the bully stuttered.

"Not you, you stupid kid!" Principal Goodburn snapped, stroking Blinky on the head. "Now get out of here. Blinky needs his rest, don't you, Blinky? YES you DO!"

It's sick really, Michael thought. He exchanged a confused look with Jasper and Grumpy Old Ms. Jones. They walked out without a word. *I just don't know why that man is employed.* He hung his head, upset that his getaway had been foiled. *Now I'm going to have to wait until recess....Or do I?*

"Um....Grumpy Old Ms. Jones?...I mean, Ms. Jones?" he asked.

"Yes, Michael, what is it?" she said dismissively, deep in thought.

"We haven't missed the Pledge of Allegiance, have we? I mean, shouldn't we be heading towards the flagpole?"

"Flagpole! Of course! I don't think we have, although it's almost impossible to determine how long we were in there," she said, looking down at her watch and tapping it.

"It's like time stopped," Michael said to Jasper under his breath.

"Don't talk to me," the bully said. "Whatever happened in there stays in there. For one, I'm too scared. And two, I'm not a nice guy. Do you hear me? I'm NOT a nice guy."

Whatever, Michael thought. *I know what I heard. And saw. And stuff.*

But he was too preoccupied thinking about how to save Doc to worry about it. Now was his chance! But how?

When they got outside they found the whole school around the flagpole. Michael looked for Crispin, but didn't see her.

Maybe I imagined the whole thing? Garbage!

When they met up with his class, he had a crazy thought. *These kids look a whole year older*! he thought. *Middle school is weird.* Grumpy Old Ms. Jones thanked one of the other teachers for watching her students and directed their attention to the pole in the center of the circle. That's when the whispering began.

"Is that a rabbit?" someone asked.

"No way that's a rabbit, that's a dinosaur!" said someone else.

It's my friend, Michael thought sadly.

He looked at Doc. The rabbit looked miserable. *What can I do?* he wondered. Scratching his head, he went through all of the possibilities, not ruling out going back in time. *Aha!* he thought excitedly.

Impulsively, Michael ran towards the flagpole.

"Doc!" he yelled, tripping and falling into a puddle of mud.

The school gasped as one, unsure of what to make of the unusual scene. This wasn't an ordinary Thursday after all. Children everywhere began to scream. Some cheering Michael on, others just because they liked being loud. The teachers tried to calm everyone down with little success. It was nuts! Just pure nuts! Like, roasted nuts, but not roasted. Burnt nuts. Crazy nuts.

His face splattered with mud, Michael reached out to Doc. The rabbit cried, gasping for air as the rope tightened around his neck.

What? Michael wondered. *We should have learned sign language or something.*

Suddenly, a girl ran out of the crowd towards him. *Crispin!* he thought excitedly. She was almost to the flagpole when she was stopped by Grumpy Old Ms. Jones.

"Already causing trouble at your new school?" Ms. Jones said, pulling Crispin back. "I wouldn't do that if I were you, Miss Rye."

Michael's heart sank. Crispin looked at him and mouthed "Sorry" before she disappeared in the crowd. *At least she tried,* he thought. *No one else is doing anything!*

All of the other teachers besides Grumpy Old Ms. Jones had given up trying to restore order. Some were messaging on their phones. Others were standing around talking, hoping that the situation would resolve itself.

(They weren't great problem solvers to be honest...)

Suddenly, a slender man in a clean white coat walked through the crowd and into the circle.

"Animal services here. I got a call about a deranged rabbit on the premises from an unknown caller. Is this the deranged rabbit, ma'am?" he said, addressing Ms. Jones with a thick country accent. Michael felt like he knew that man from somewhere, but he couldn't put a finger on it.

"Well, I don't know who called you, but you're a lifesaver," Ms. Jones said. "We don't know where this rabbit came from, but he's caused quite a stir here in our morning assembly. Thank you so much for taking him off our hands. I hope he finds a nice home with you."

"You're welcome, ma'am, I'm just doing my job. We'll make sure he gets back on his feet," the man chuckled, smiling at them.

Michael watched in horror. *I can't make my move now, I'll never make it. Who did this?* But he already knew. Dapply. *Drat! He's trying to separate us,* he thought, angrily. *He's got something evil up his sleeve!*

Just then, Principal Goodburn bolted out of the school.

"Wait!! Wait!!" he yelled rushing toward them. "You can't take that animal! I'm the principal at this school. Every decision has to come through me, Jerry Mudwater!"

Another Jerry? Whoa, Michael thought. *They're everywhere!!!!*

"Now, Principal Goodburn, I've only been out of your school for five years, but I know a thing or two about animals and this one's rabid."

No, he's not! Michael wanted to say.

"No, he's not!" Principal Goodburn said angrily.

Whoa, thanks! Michael didn't like the man, but he had to admire his courage. At least he was standing up for Doc.

"Rabid or not, don't you think he deserves a proper home? Here with me perhaps?" Principal Goodburn said, twitching with excitement. "After all, everybody knows that you're just going to kill him when you get back to the shelter."

Kill him?!?!?! Michael gasped. The crowd looked at Jerry accusingly.

"Now Lionel, you and I both know that's not true!" Jerry drawled, ruffling his mullet uncomfortably. When that didn't satisfy the crowd, he stroked his goatee and continued. "And even so, I'm not sure I would give you another animal. After all, I don't think you're quite in code as is. I should report you to the county, you know?"

"Why, Mr. Mudwater, I don't know what you mean?" Principal Goodburn chuckled, shifting side to side uneasily. He seemed eager to change the subject. "And since when have you called me Lionel?" He looked around at the crowd and squeaked.

"Since I had a job to do," Jerry said firmly.

"But I...I..."

Principal Goodburn looked like a stalk of celery drained of its juice. Taking one last look at Doc, he turned around and ran back into the school.

"I'm just glad to see some things don't change," Jerry laughed, pulling Doc down from the flagpole. "Give my respects to the family, ma'am, this one's safe with me."

He nodded to Ms. Jones and placed Doc in a small cage in the back of his truck. Waving at the children one last time, he sped away into the distance, taking Michael's friend with him.

"Well, I'm glad that's over," Grumpy Old Ms. Jones said, relieved. "I think we should skip flagpole today."

The rest of the school murmured in agreement and began walking toward their classrooms. Michael stood up, looking longingly at the road.

"Need help?" Jasper asked, shuffling beside him.

"With what?"

"This!" the bully said, pushing him back over. The contents of Michael's fanny pack spilled out onto the ground.

Michael glared at him, wishing that Crispin was nearby.

"Sucker!" Jasper yelled, grabbing some of Michael's stuff and getting lost in the crowd.

What a jerk. I hope he didn't take anything important, Michael thought.

But as he began to put everything back into his fanny pack he realized he was wrong. Really dead wrong. I don't know how to emphasize this enough to you. HE WAS WRONG! Pretty much everything he needed was there (the Vanilla Squares were no loss) except for one thing.

The book!

At first he couldn't decide why he was upset. After all, the book didn't seem to contain anything but a really confusing riddle and a bunch of blank pages. No loss there. But Doc seemed to think it was important and that made Michael wonder. What if he couldn't defeat Lord Piper now because he didn't have it? He shuddered to think of what Jasper would do with it.

He'll probably make paper airplanes out of it or something. Not that I hadn't considered it, but I have to get it back! he gasped.

After all, something about it had to justify the mysterious frog's actions. Otherwise, why would he have taken him away from the feast and not given him a chance to save his friends? He knew that Lord Piper was coming, didn't he? And why was Doc willing to die to protect it?

Was it really that important? Was it really about Lord Piper?

Michael was the last one to arrive back to the classroom and was called on as he sat down. Crispin smiled at him from across the room.

"Michael, do you know the answer?" Grumpy Old Ms. Jones asked.

Come on, really? he thought. *A question? She totally knows I just came in late and I don't even have the homework assignment because I haven't been here. Who does that? She's been so nice. Oh well.*

Thinking really hard about what they might be studying he decided to guess. "Umm...the War of 1812?" he answered.

The class laughed. Apparently, he'd guessed wrong.

Ms. Jones smiled. "While that's a great answer for a lot of other questions Michael, it doesn't have anything to do with what we're talking about right now."

"Atticus Finch?" he guessed again, although he was sure that sixth grade was a little too early to be reading 'To Kill a Mockingbird.'

"No Michael, it was math. Maybe you should ask Jasper to help you. He's been so studious this year."

That's because he's like eighteen, Michael thought.

He looked over at the bully and saw him with his head down, apparently attempting to read something. He'd pulled his desk up behind Tommy Snaggletooth, presumably to cheat, leaving a giant space behind him.

Of course he's doing well. Tommy's like the smartest boy in the class! Michael shook his head. *What is that Jasper's reading? Oh,* he thought, realizing his mistake. *Confound it!*

Jasper wasn't expecting him to attack, not here, so that's exactly what Michael did. Jumping out of his chair, he tackled the bully, knocking him to the floor and taking Tommy Snaggletooth with him. Unsure of what had happened, Jasper began punching wildly into the air, knocking Tommy out almost immediately.

Screaming, Ms. Jones rushed to the back of the room to break them up, but couldn't get close enough without being hit herself. Dragging Tommy out of further harm, she yelled at one of the students to get help.

Jasper was still holding the book out of reach when Principal Goodburn arrived with Suzie. *Really?* Michael thought. *Something about this guy has to be illegal.* But he wasn't going to argue with teeth that size so he let go and backed up. He noticed he was crying.

"You can cry all you want, Mr. Pumpernickel, but this is your fault and you know it," Principal Goodburn said with a disapproving look.

Michael was more worried about what Suzie was thinking. It might have been his imagination, but she looked hungry. *Me too*, he thought.

"It's rare that I have the same students in my office twice in one day," he continued. "But somehow it doesn't surprise me that it's you two. Let's go," he said gesturing them along. Suzie growled at Michael as he stood up and walked to the front of the classroom. Grumpy Old Ms. Jones thanked Principal Goodburn and asked if there was anything she could do to repay him.

"How about dinner? My place?" he said excitedly. "Tonight! And tomorrow! We can eat sushi!" He was literally bouncing in place.

"Wouldn't that um...violate the school's policy about relationships outside of the classroom between the administration and the sixth grade teaching staff?" she answered, hoping he hadn't actually read the rule book. She didn't know what it said, but it wasn't likely to be so specific. She just didn't want to spend any more time with Lionel than she had to. Plus she had Boris to think about, after all.

Principal Goodburn paused for a moment, then looked disappointed. "Yes, I guess you're right, Margaret. Sweet, sweet Margaret. Well, we're even then."

Turning away to hide his own tears, he pushed Michael and Jasper out of the room and ushered them to his office.

Great, not here again, Michael thought. *Maybe it won't be so bad this time,* he reassured himself.

But he was wrong. Kind of like always, he's not really good at that kind of thing is he? Oh well. When they got to the office there was someone waiting for them.

It was the last person Michael wanted to see.

"Mr. Clemmons, thank you so much for coming!" Principal Goodburn said, sitting down at his desk and pouring a cup of tea. He motioned for the boys to sit on the floor and directed his attention to Dapply who sat before them wearing a different suit than this morning.

Figures, Michael thought.

Looking down at the floor, he decided to stand in the corner furthest from Suzie's cage instead.

"I'm so glad you got my call because you see I'm very concerned about the relationship between your son Jasper and Mr. Pumpernickel here."

"As am I," Dapply insisted, glaring at Jasper.

"I want you to know, Mr. Clemmons, that fighting or intimidating others is not acceptable in this school. It reflects badly on all of us and could even prevent a certain principal from winning the upcoming state superintendant election this November. It will NOT be tolerated!" he yelled, slamming his fist down on his desk.

"I could not agree more, Principal Goodburn. This is not like my son at all," Dapply said.

Right, Michael thought. *Usually, he's beaten up more kids by this time of day.*

"So I want you to be the first to know that I may have to recommend, how do you say this, alternative forms of discipline?" Principal Goodburn said tersely.

What? Michael panicked. *Why isn't MY dad here?*

"And I want you to know that I support whatever it is that you need to do, Allen."

"Thank you, Mr. Clemmons, but it's Lionel."

"My mistake."

"It's just so refreshing," Principal Goodburn continued, "to hear of a parent who wants the best for their son. A disciplined boy makes a disciplined man. I have all of these animals in here for a reason, you know," he chuckled. Dapply smiled an evil smile.

"Of course."

Michael and Jasper looked at each other and then at the array of cages around them. They wouldn't even stand a chance against the fish.

"But Allen," Dapply continued. "Don't you think it would be best to try something else first? Perhaps," he paused. "...it would be best for the boys to talk it out over lunch? I could take them to Sombrero Sid's? Even pay for Mr. Pumpernickel's meal. You should really let me do that if you know what's good for you," he added.

"Why, Mr. Clemmons, you don't have to do that!" Principal Goodburn said, looking uncomfortable.

Really, you don't have to do that, Michael thought.

It was going to be really hard to work his way out of this one. A lunch date with the class bully and his biggest enemy. He didn't want that.

Even if it WAS lunch.

"Oh, but I do, Allen, I do! Obviously, this incident is the result of some sort of parenting failure of mine. And Mr. Pumpernickel here clearly doesn't even have parents who care enough to show up to this meeting," Dapply said.

"You didn't even invite them!" Michael yelled.

Slightly shaken, Principal Goodburn ignored Michael and directed his attention to Dapply who passed him something under the desk. "I think that would be a fantastic idea, Mr. Clemmons," he said winking at them. "Take the boys to lunch, I'll let Margaret know. You don't even have to bring Mr. Pumpernickel back until the end of the day!"

Or never, more likely, Michael thought.

Fear filled his heart. Principal Goodburn had been bought off. That was the only way to explain the sudden change of direction. Michael had been so worried about saving Doc that he'd walked into a trap of his own. Now they were BOTH doomed.

"Well, it's settled then!" Dapply said, eying Michael victoriously. "Come on Jasper, Michael. Let's go eat 'lunch' together."

Michael didn't have to be in seventh grade to know that Dapply had said the word lunch in quotes. That meant that they weren't really going to eat lunch. Which was a bummer since he WAS really hungry.

Jasper practically had to drag him out of the room as they left Principal Goodburn alone to count his newfound riches. The bully was telling his dad how excited he was to be skipping school, but Dapply ignored him, relishing the moment.

"Victory is sweet, Michael Pumpernickel. Like the extra cream on a chocolate layer cake. You can only imagine the reward that I will receive when I deliver you to Lord Piper. The riches. The glory," he laughed. "Jasper, go back to class," he said suddenly, turning to his son.

"What?!" the bully asked, disappointed.

"There's been a change of plans, son," he said. Suddenly, he saw the book in Jasper's hands. "And what is this?" he asked.

"I...I don't know Dad," Jasper said. "I stole it from Michael."

"Did you?" Dapply said, his eyes lighting up. "Well why don't you let me borrow this. After all, you won't have time while you're in class. What with all of those books and such. Not that you can read anyway," he chuckled.

Things just keep getting worse, Michael thought.

Not knowing what else to do, Jasper handed the book to his father and walked back to class. Dapply flipped through the pages, confused, but satisfied, putting it beneath his arm.

"You look tired, Michael," he said as they approached a different car than the organist had driven that morning. Michael was feeling a lot of things, but tired wasn't one of them.

Scared. Not not scared. Does that cover it?

"No?" Dapply asked, trying to sound surprised. "Are you sure? You can't possibly be sure, can you?"

"You won't get very far," Michael said under his breath. "There's a search team looking for me. And once my friends find out what happened, they'll look for me too."

Dapply laughed. "But Michael...any search team would be broken up. You've been found! How do you know that they were on your side, anyway?"

Ummm....

"And as for your friends? Well, I don't think the rabbit will be going anywhere anytime soon," he said smiling. "You know, your porcupine friend is in over his head. He really doesn't know what he's gotten himself into, that traitor. Chet won't help you either. Surely you know that! Face it. You're Lord Piper's now."

Michael fought the urge to cry out. He really had no idea what to do. Were all of his friends really traitors? Was he fighting against Lord Piper alone? Maybe taking a nap wouldn't be such a bad idea after all.

(It never is!)

"Seriously, Michael, I think you need a nap!" Dapply insisted.

Michael was about to answer him when Dapply's right hand found his face. He blacked out.

So that's where Jasper learned it! Michael thought.

When he woke up his head was pounding. *It's like a thousand guys with really big drumsticks are hitting me right now. And it doesn't matter if it's the chicken kind of drumstick or the wood kind of drumstick either!*

Michael tried to remember where he was, but he couldn't. He certainly wasn't at school. Or WAS he? So far he didn't like sixth grade. Looking around, all he saw was darkness and it made him incredibly nervous.

Nap time is wayyyyyyyy different than when I was in kindergarten...Man, it's hot in here.

He gasped for air and gagged on something in his mouth. *What the junk?!?!*

Unable to breathe, he lashed around, but found that his hands and feet were tied. *Where am I?* he screamed, although it came out as little more than a whimper. There was no escape from the darkness. He was trapped. The lack of air began to make him dizzy even though he'd managed to push the gag out of his mouth with his tongue.

The more he struggled, the tighter the bands on his hands and feet became. He wasn't just dying, he realized. He was like...killing himself!

Suddenly, Michael felt something crawl across his leg. He wasn't sure what it was, but it felt cold and rough to the touch. Jerking in surprise, he felt blood trickle down his back as the rope cut into his wrists. The thought of something else with him, wherever he was, did little to ease his fears. Whatever its purpose, he didn't think the creature was here to keep him company.

Then, just as before, he felt it crawl across him again. Tensing up, Michael panicked, knocking his head against something hard. Every bone in his body screamed in agony.

Whatever that thing is, it needs to go away! It's not helping.

But then suddenly, as if to prove him wrong, the knots on his arms and legs loosened. He could feel something being removed from his head slowly.

CHAPTER 30

Looking down, he found his hands and feet untied.

Well, that's awesome!

His eyes slowly adjusted to the darkness as he looked around. The room he was in was barely big enough for a child his size, much less an adult. Trunk-size almost. Plotting an escape was out of the question.

"I'm in his car?" Michael wondered aloud.

"Tada! Congratulations! You get a gold star!" Dapply exclaimed from the front seat. "But you see...I'm afraid you'll have to find a gold star yourself. I'm up here and you're back there and well, there's no way I'm stopping the car before I get to Lord Piper unless I have to. That would be...how do I say it? Ill-advised."

Michael didn't answer him.

"Oh, it's okay. You figured it out faster than I thought you would! Maybe you're not a dense as my little Jasper says you are."

"Little Jasper?" He said I'm dense? Michael thought incredulously.

He almost laughed out loud. But he was determined not to give Dapply the satisfaction of an answer. Instead, he racked his mind to try and figure out how his bonds had become loose.

"I'm sure by now you're wondering why I tied you up. The rope is probably already digging into your bones," Dapply laughed. "But I want to assure you that it's for your safety. No, you're not going blind either. There's a bag on your head! Yes, it IS the same kind the government uses in interrogations and no, don't ask me where I got it."

Michael accidently bumped into the roof of the trunk as he turned around. What had untied his ropes? Was it whatever touched his leg? If so, then he probably owed it an apology for all the bad words he'd thought of. He'd even used some for the first time!

Dapply however took this sound as one of affirmation and continued talking to himself.

"Now Michael, you're embarrassing me!" he exclaimed. "Of course I'm the greatest super villain. There's no need for you to say that, but it certainly is nice of you."

I said no such thing.

"But I couldn't agree more. After all, do you think I'm really going to let Lord Piper win? Why, he's a fox! I'm a human. He wears sunglasses! I don't even have contacts.

It's already insulting enough to have to listen to his every command, much less obey them. Sure, he was pretty convincing when he first came to me, but who would turn down the offer I got? No one!" Dapply said laughing. "Can you keep a secret, Michael? After I turn you over to Lord Piper, I'm going to skin him alive. Why, you might ask? Because I'll need a new rug for my mansion. I've done most of the work anyway. He never could have persuaded that old fool Goddard to lead you to me."

Ohhhhhh, Michael thought. *So he IS after me too.* Suddenly, the one-man search party didn't seem so threatening. He'd seen Goddard's gun cabinet.

"Get out of the way!" Dapply yelled, interrupting Michael's thoughts.

Without warning, the car struck something large and careened off the road. Michael hit his head on the roof and landed on something sharp. He quickly rolled off the object to see what it was.

"Grohill?" he whispered. The porcupine gave him a thumbs up (however animals do that) and a smile, but motioned for Michael to keep quiet.

"Oh yeah, Dapply's still here!" Michael said.

"You're darn right I'm still here. Where do you think I would have gone? Topeka?" Dapply said, clearly irritated. "Now, I need your help to get me out this ditch. I hope those stupid kids learned their lesson."

WHAT? He hit children? Michael thought horrified. *Wait...He's going to let me out of the trunk?*

"Now if you think I'm going to let you out of the trunk then you're just as crazy as that kid whose wagon I hit. I need you to shift your weight to the back of the car. It'll probably work because you're HUGE. Can you do that for me, Michael? You can, can't you? Because if you don't, well...." Dapply laughed. "Let's just say you might make it to Lord Piper...over time."

His happiness of escape short-lived, Michael was glad to hear Dapply hadn't hit anybody. He was worried he would have been charged just for being in the car.

Because that could totally happen. You never know.

"I'll try," Michael said nervously.

"If you don't do more than that you might be wearing your last set of clothes, boy!"

At least I'm in my favorite shirt...

265

Dapply revved the car's engine and they shot out of the ditch onto the road. Cars honked as they sped down the highway, the wagon caught in the back.

"Well that wasn't so hard, was it?" Dapply said. "Although, Jasper told me you've got a lot of weight to throw around."

Now Jasper's saying I'M big? What's going on? Michael thought angrily. *Big is in his name!*

The sound of the wagon hitting the road made a screeching noise much like fingernails on the chalkboard. It was giving Michael a headache. Like he didn't have enough problems. But their troubles weren't over yet. It wasn't long before the car started to lurch back and forth, the engine sputtering.

"Oh, blast it all! That stupid wagon must have done something to the car. Good thing it's not mine, I stole it from Widow Allen. It looks like we WILL be stopping before I get you to Lord Piper. I'm pulling into a service station now. Don't try any funny business."

Michael looked at Grohill. Both of them knew what Dapply meant by 'funny business' and that's exactly what they were going to do.

When the car stopped they went into action. Pushing hard on the seat in front of them, they were banking on the fact that Widow Allen's car was like the one Ralph had shoved Michael into as a kid. They heard Dapply arguing with someone outside, but the voices faded.

"They must have gone inside, this is our chance!" Michael said.

Grohill nodded and they gave it one last push.

Victory!

They crawled across the seat and through the side door. Michael looked inside and saw that Dapply was in a heated argument with one of the repairmen.

"Of course there's a wagon attached to the back of my car," he yelled. "No, I don't know how it got there. Does that even matter? How long is it going to take?" He glanced back at the car, paying special attention to the trunk.

"Quick! This way!" Michael whispered.

Somehow, Dapply didn't see them as they darted across the parking lot and over the road into the woods. Michael smiled.

When they got to the woods, Michael was breathing hard. He wanted to sleep, but first he wanted some answers. From the look of it, they'd been driving for a few hours and the sun was beginning to sink below the trees.

"Dapply told me you're a traitor," Michael said softly. "I don't want to believe him, but you haven't given me any reason not to. Hitting Doc. Running away. Not helping a friend. How do I know I can trust you?"

Grohill began to cry. Michael had seen this before in a soap opera he wasn't supposed to watch when he was home sick from school one day. The porcupine was looking for sympathy. He was dodging the question. This made Michael angry.

"Don't give me that, you filthy rodent!" he yelled, knocking Grohill up against a tree.

His anger surprised him, but what right did Grohill have to cry? If anybody did, HE did!

"I'm...I'm so sorry, Master Michael. I really am. Please don't call me names! I heard what Dapply said about me. I was there, remember?"

Suddenly Michael felt bad. Of course Grohill had been there! He was the reason they had escaped!

"I didn't mean it that way, I'm sorry!" Michael said still shaking. "It's just that...I guess when you're being chased by a crazy old man with a gun, a search party with a gun and a well-dressed parent of one of your classmates, it's important to figure out who your friends are. After all, I'm not even really sure what I'm doing here. Why is Lord Piper after me? I don't want to fight him!"

Grohill grinned through his tears. "But Master Michael," he said, "it's about the legends. Surely you know that by now?"

"I mean, I know what I've been told. At least what I've heard. But why me? Why am I the Chosen One? I'm just a dude. Nothing special. I don't even know any animals that can talk. Well..." he said, looking at Grohill. "I didn't."

"Master Michael, there's a story I heard when I was young. It was about a superhero and his oversized bald eagle, Jefferson."

"Sneaky Pete?"

I thought he didn't know about Sneaky Pete...

"Yeah, that's the one!" Grohill said, his eyes lighting up. "Now Sneaky Pete and Jefferson were best friends. Inseparable from the very moment they met. One day, the Great Spook turned them on each other and they didn't know who to trust."

I don't remember that issue, Michael thought, confused. *And I know every issue.* "What happened?"

"They decided not to listen to other people. They were friends, just like we are, Michael. That was more important than anything anybody else had to say! We're still the Fearless Band of Outcasts, aren't we?"

Michael frowned. Grohill hadn't answered the question OR apologized for what he'd done to Doc. Michael wanted answers. But he really loved Sneaky Pete too so he figured it could wait.

"Yeah we are!" he said smiling.

And the two friends laid down in the remaining sunlight and drifted off to sleep.

When Michael woke up he was hungry. REALLY hungry. Grohill was still asleep so he thought he would wander into town to find some food. *I'll be back before he wakes up anyway,* he thought.

They hadn't traveled far into the woods so it was only a matter of time before he was back at the highway again. Apparently, a few hours had passed since they'd gone to sleep because it was dark.

What time is it? he wondered.

(Time to get a watch! Just kidding...)

Looking both ways before crossing the road (as any responsible young man would), Michael recognized the service station from earlier in the day. Dapply's car was gone! This made him smile.

I wonder if he's noticed I'm not there, he chuckled. Michael looked up the hill and saw a place called Hungry

Woody's. He'd never been to one of those before! From what he could tell, it served food and that's all that mattered. When he arrived in front of Woody's, the scent of freshly grilled burgers almost knocked him over.

"I think I'm going to like Hungry Woody's," he said excitedly.

The place actually looked pretty gross, but the fear of poor sanitation wasn't going to stop him now, it never did. Pushing the door open, he was greeted by a wall of smoke. When it cleared, he saw two men arguing at a bar.

"This is definitely not a family establishment," he coughed.

(You might be right...)

But apparently no one had told Hungry Woody's that. He was greeted by a singing, smiling cow who showed him to his seat. The other customers were staring at him.

Maybe they weren't lucky enough to get the cow? he thought. *Either that, or they're jealous of my fanny pack. Not that I'm going to apologize for that.*

Michael didn't plan on telling the cow he didn't have any money until after he'd eaten. Probably a good call. He was distressed to find out that the cow wasn't his waiter. Jerry Mudwater from animal control was.

"Welcome to Hungry Woody's, home of the Hungry Woody Mile-High challenge. My name is Jerry. I'll be your server. What do you want?" he said, avoiding eye contact with Michael.

Evidently, animal control didn't pay their employees very well. Either that or Jerry had this job because he liked it. That didn't seem to be the case.

Michael was overwhelmed by the menu. There were almost 16 pages of burgers alone! Somehow it just felt wrong eating one in the cow's presence, but he decided he really wanted one and could distract it when the time came.

"Well, are you ready or do you want me to come back when I've grown a beard?" Jerry said.

He already has a goatee! Michael thought, although he was a little worried about Jerry's mullet, which might get into his food.

You have to watch out for mullets.

"I'll have the triple-pickle five-pound, mutton glutton big time burger with the garlic fries," he answered.

273

"Whatever," Jerry said and started to walk off. He paused and turned to face Michael. "Wait a second," he said, a look of recognition crossing his face. "Aren't you the kid from that school this morning who made my job so gosh darn hard?"

Michael shook his head. Jerry considered it for a moment and walked off.

"That was easy," Michael said, relieved. Jerry hadn't even asked if he had any money!

"Now I don't usually do this, you see," Jerry began, suddenly reappearing behind Michael. "But I don't ordinarily serve children alone this late at night. Or ever really. You're going to have to tell me where your parents are or I can't serve you. We might have to wait until they get here." He eyed Michael suspiciously.

Michael froze. *Maybe I could call them and they could give him permission over the phone?* he wondered. But he knew it wouldn't work. They were probably out looking for him anyway. He didn't want them to find him so that might be a bad idea.

"It's okay, Jerry, he's a friend," a girl said, walking over to Michael's table. Jerry shrugged and walked away.

"Crispin!" he gasped. "What are you doing here?"

She had traded her regular t-shirt for a 'Hungry Woody's' one. It hung loosely above her jeans.

"I come here every night," she said. "My Dad owns this place!"

I won't hold that against you, Michael thought.

"But, Michael," she said, concerned. "What happened to you at school today? Where did you go? I can't believe you stood up to that bully! You were so brave!"

Michael puffed his chest with pride. "Oh, it was nothing. I explained it to Principal Goodburn and he let me have the rest of the day off."

He was uncomfortable lying to Crispin, but he figured if he wanted someone to like him it was best to not mention evil foxes and talking animals right away.

"Oh," she said, confused. "Well, I'm glad you're not hurt! I was thinking about you all day."

Michael smiled. "Thanks!"

Crispin grinned back. They sat in silence for a few minutes. But it wasn't the awkward kind that Michael was so desperate to avoid. They were just enjoying each other's company.

So THIS is what this is like...

"I like your fanny pack," Crispin said finally.

"You do?" Michael asked, confused. "Everyone says that I'm a nerd for carrying it."

"Well, they're wrong," she said. "How else are you going to be able to carry your entire Hedgemon collection with you? What if you didn't have the holographic Roongbob someone wanted in exchange for a Whoopsy?"

"Exactly!" Michael said excitedly. "That's what I keep telling people."

"Well, you keep telling them, Michael. One day they'll believe you. I do."

"Crispin!" a voice yelled from the kitchen.

"Uh oh, that's my Dad," Crispin said sadly, a look of longing in her eyes. "It was nice to see you, Michael."

"I hope I see you later, Crispin," Michael said, disappointed that she had to leave. Crispin got up and left Michael at the table alone with his thoughts.

She's perfect, he thought. *I can't believe I would say this, but I might just love her more than Miss Dandelion.*

Suddenly, a couple two tables away caught his eye. They were facing the stage and talking excitedly about the band that was about to play.

As chance would have it, the band was Minotaur.

Let's see if Boris was right about them, Michael thought. But he couldn't stop staring at the couple. *They look so familiar...*

"Ralph!" he said, jumping up from the table and crashing to the floor. His brother turned around, a confused expression on his face.

"Michael?" Ralph asked. "What are you doing here? You're not supposed to be out this late! Mom and Dad are looking for you everywhere! I think they've even got Prometheus with them." Ralph was furious.

So they ARE looking for me. Cool.

"I was kidnapped!" Michael blurted out before his instincts told him not to. Suddenly, the restaurant became quiet. Very quiet. And everyone had their eyes on Michael and Ralph. Even the cow, naturally.

"Don't be stupid, you weren't kidnapped, Michael," Ralph said angrily. "Mom told me you were at school today, but then you left. You're going to be in big trouble when we get home. I can't believe I'm doing this." He offered Michael a hand.

Michael took it and stood up. To his relief, the crowd started to talk again. But there was no way he was going to leave now. He was HUNGRY.

"I'm not going anywhere, especially with you!" he said taking Ralph by surprise. "I need to eat. When I'm done I'm going back to the forest to see if Grohill's up."

"Grohill? Forest? What ARE you talking about? Now you're going to tell me you're not here alone. Is your invisible friend Oliver with you? This is unbelievable." Ralph's face had turned a deep red.

Oh yeah, Oliver. I hadn't thought about him! Maybe if I called him, he could get here soon. Then HE could pay. Then again, Oliver has been extremely unreliable recently. I'm just not sure I can count on him to show up anymore. Even though he never shows up because he's invisible...

"Go easy on him, Ralph, he's been through a lot. Can you imagine being lost?"

Michael turned and saw his piano teacher sitting across the table from his brother. "Miss Dandelion?!?!?!" he gasped.

"Yes, Michael. I wouldn't have expected Ralph to tell you," she said, suddenly irritated. "But your brother and I are dating."

No!

Her expression softened and she grabbed Ralph's hand. Ralph looked at her and smiled. "We came here to see the band, but it's past your bedtime," she said.

"Alice is right, Michael, let's go home," Ralph sighed taking his brother's hand and leading him toward the door.

"But...but I didn't get any food! Aren't you going to stay for the show? What a rip-off! You can't do this to me! You're being so unfair! What are you doing?" Michael was going bats.

"We'll grab you something at Sombrero Sid's on the way home. Besides, they just announced Minotaur's lead singer can't make it because of car troubles or something."

Suddenly, Jerry Mudwater walked onto the stage.

"Folks, I have some good news," he said. "It looks like the lead singer IS here after all. My mistake." He collapsed off the stage, falling into a table full of mean looking biker guys.

The biker guys did not respond to the situation well.

He looks tired...Maybe we SHOULD get out of here, this could get ugly, Michael thought.

The audience cheered, ignoring Jerry, as the band took the platform. Miss Dandelion and Ralph paused, finding a corner by the entrance.

"Staying for one song won't hurt anyone, will it?" Miss Dandelion smiled, looking down at Michael. He wasn't so sure.

"Hellooooo Woody's!" Minotaur's lead singer yelled jumping onto the stage. "Are you ready to rockkkkkk?!?!?"

I'm ready to rock, Michael thought, absorbed in the moment. *I've never been to a rock concert before!*

He looked around for Crispin, hoping that she could see how cool he was, but she must have been in the back. This looked like his kind of band too. The lead singer was wearing a seersucker suit with a pink bow tie! His straw hat was pulled over his eyes ever-so-slightly in a way that made him look dangerous.

Wait a second. I've seen this guy somewhere. And those two other guys too.

He racked his brain, but he couldn't remember. He was too hungry! Miss Dandelion and Ralph seemed to be enjoying the concert so he decided to forget about it. Suddenly, the band stopped mid-song.

Dapply stared at him wide-eyed from the stage. The audience looked around confused until their eyes settled on Michael.

"Change of plans. This concert is over!" Dapply said, excitedly.

Holy crow, he's everywhere! And the Twins are back!

Michael bolted through the door and into the parking lot. Ralph was close behind, dragging Miss Dandelion with him.

"Michael, WHAT ARE YOU DOING?!?!?" Ralph yelled, chasing him down the hill. "STOP!" But Michael needed every second he could get.

"Michael, please slow down. What's going on?" Miss Dandelion yelled. She looked furious. Her Minotaur shirt, with Dapply's smiling face on it, somehow seemed inadequate as it began to rain.

Michael had never seen her like this before, even when he had touched the pedal on her piano with his bare foot. He didn't like it, but he didn't have a choice. Unless you know, he wanted to die. Plus, he liked Crispin now!

"I can't tell you!" he yelled. "But I can show you. Watch out!"

Ralph and Miss Dandelion turned around to see Dapply and the Twins close behind, gaining on their already slim lead.

"The guys from the band?" Ralph yelled, grabbing Miss Dandelion's hand and picking up his pace. "Really, Michael? What HAVE you been doing?"

They darted across the road, narrowly avoiding the oncoming traffic. Dapply and the Twins, however were not quite as lucky. As they dove into the woods they heard the sound of screeching tires followed by a deafening bang. That's not usually a good thing. In case, it was ALSO not a good thing. Oh well...

"I hope they're okay," Miss Dandelion frowned.

"If they're dead, I can't get autographs," Ralph said.

"I don't care what happens to them!" Michael said angrily. "Quick, keep moving!"

"No, Michael," Ralph said grabbing his brother's arm and stopping him dead in his tracks. "Look. Someone's chasing you. I get it. But you can't expect us to help you if we don't know what's going on. We can't."

"Please tell us what's wrong, Michael. Why was that band chasing you?"

It didn't look like he had any other options. "I'll tell you," Michael said, breathing hard. "But first, you have to do something about that shirt!"

"Michael! That's very inappropriate. Please tell Alice that you're sorry."

"That's not what I meant! It's just....Can we walk while I tell you?" he asked.

They nodded.

"Umm...so you know the guy in the band? That was the guy that captured me at school today...."

He told them everything. He told them about the creepy letter and Lord Piper. He told them about Sneaks the rabbit and Old Man Goddard. He told them about the village and Mortimer's death. He even told them about Chet and Doc being taken away. (He didn't tell them about Crisipin in case Miss Dandelion would get upset)

And when he was finished, he looked up and took a deep breath. They were staring at him like he had three heads!

"That was a really nice story, Michael," Miss Dandelion said. A look of concern spread across her face.

Ralph paused to gather his thoughts. "You know what, Michael?"

"What?" Michael asked, hoping Ralph believed him.

"It WAS a nice story," Ralph laughed, punching Michael playfully on the shoulder. "You should think about writing a book. How do you make this stuff up? That was great," he said.

Michael's heart sank. *Crispin would believe me.* "So you think I made that up?" he asked.

"Wait," Ralph paused. "You weren't kidding?"

Michael wanted to cry, but he wasn't sure he could do it in front of Miss Dandelion. He kept walking.

"Michael, wait!" she yelled, chasing him.

"What?" Ralph asked. "What did I do?" Shaking his head, he ran after them, his stomach churning from the triple pickle, mutton glutton, big time burger he'd eaten. Apparently, Michael was lucky he hadn't eaten...

Michael finally stopped when they came to a large clearing. In the middle, Grohill was pacing furiously.

"Oh where could he be? Where could he be? Oh my, oh my, now I've done it! I've lost him. I knew I shouldn't have trusted those other guys. Oh my, oh my..."

He was hitting himself over the head with a pinecone. Ralph and Miss Dandelion stood in shock, their mouths hanging open. Michael on the other hand, laughed.

"If you hit yourself on the head with that pinecone hard enough, you might become a tree!" he said.

Surprised, Grohill turned and ran towards Michael, embracing him. Michael grimaced as the spikes pierced the undersides of his arms. Nothing could break his good spirit though. He'd escaped Dapply and now Ralph would have no choice but to believe him! Suddenly noticing the others, Grohill jumped behind Michael.

As if on cue, Ralph pointed at where Grohill had been. "Wh...what IS that?"

"I could ask you the same thing," Grohil snapped stepping forward. "Michael?"

"Is this some sort of trick?" Ralph said, kneeling down to eye level with Grohill. The porcupine shrieked and ran into the bushes.

"Great, Ralph. Seriously. Now you've done it!" Miss Dandelion said disapprovingly.

Ralph glared at her, glancing back at the bush. "Done what, Alice? We don't even know what that thing was!" He tossed a pinecone in Grohill's direction.

"That *thing* is a porcupine," Michael said stepping in between them. "And he's my friend, so be nice to him!"

Ralph looked disgusted. "What do you mean that thing is your friend? Did you see it hitting its head back there? It's crazy!"

"HE'S distressed," Michael said. "And I think you're making him feel even worse." The bush was rattling back and forth with Grohill's sobs. Miss Dandelion looked on with sympathy.

"This is ridiculous," Ralph said, his face turning red. "First you crash our date. Then you lead us on some crazy chase into the forest where you tell us a stupid story about talking animals. Then you even go as far as to try to make us believe they actually exist."

"But they DO exist, isn't that obvious? My friend Doc is in trouble! He was taken to an animal control facility and they kill animals there. We have to help him!"

"Oh, what is he, a koala?" Ralph laughed.

"Actually, he's a rabbit...."

"I'm sorry, a rabbit. My mistake. Whatever. Come on, Alice, let's go. We can call my parents and tell them where to find Michael."

But she didn't move. She was staring at the bush. It had stopped shaking.

"There was once a time when humans and animals talked regularly," Grohill said sadly. "A time of prosperity. A time of invention! But dark forces tore us apart. Sides were taken, promises broken. And we could no longer trust humans. So we hid, spreading lies about the forest, hoping that no one of your race would ever set foot in our home again. But a prophecy was told. One about a boy who would make things right again. That a time would come when humans and animals would live together in harmony.

We thought that you were that boy, Michael, but now I see we were wrong."

"What are you talking about, Grohill?" Michael said. "I haven't changed! Remember the Fearless Band of Outcasts? We're not here to mock you! This is my brother Ralph, he just doesn't understand."

Grohill's eyes widened. "Your brother, you say? Well, that changes everything! I thought you'd brought someone here to make fun of me. Then if you trust him, Michael, I trust him too. Who is this?" he asked, eying Miss Dandelion longingly. Evidently Michael and Grohill had more in common than they'd originally thought.

"That's Miss Dandelion, my piano teacher. She's Ralph's girlfriend."

"And a lucky guy you are," Grohill smiled, winking at Ralph. Michael's brother shifted uncomfortably and muttered something inaudible.

"Well, I'm glad we're all friends now," Miss Dandelion said, trying to change the subject. She had turned beet red, like, well, beets...

"Yeah, me too," Michael said. "Now we can save Doc!"

"Now wait a second, Michael," Ralph said. "I think I'm on board with this whole talking animals thing. I mean, I kind of have to be because there's one right in front of me. But I don't know about prophecies or crazy stuff like that. Alice has to go to work tomorrow. And you've got a lesson at 4 o'clock for that matter, not to mention school."

"That can wait, Ralph, Doc's in trouble!" Michael yelled.

Taken aback, Ralph looked at Miss Dandelion. Grohill stared at them anxiously. "There's no use reasoning with you, is there?" Ralph said cracking a smile.

"I doubt it. Reason has never been one of my strong points," Michael said, smiling back.

"Then we have a koala to save."

"Rabbit..."

"Right."

And they walked out of the woods back to Miss Dandelion's car. Dapply was gone.

After taking Miss Dandelion home, Ralph, Grohill and Michael headed to Ralph's friend Moe's house. His parents owned a costume shop and they had volunteered to loan them some costumes for the night, no questions asked.

Great parenting, Michael thought. *It's no wonder Moe's in jail.*

Grohill was especially quiet on the way over, but this gave Michael and Ralph some time to spend together, something they hadn't done in a long, long time.

"So how old are you these days, Michael?" Ralph asked.

"Seriously? You don't know how old I am?" Michael laughed, hardly surprised at his brother's incompetence. "I'm eleven." *Not that I know how old he is.*

"Oh wow, you're almost a man," Ralph said, smiling.

"I guess so."

"So everything you told me is true then? About the animals and all?"

"Everything."

"Wow," Ralph looked back at Michael. "I just....it's just that, I never pegged you as an adventure kind of guy you know? You were always such a nerd," he laughed.

"Hey!" Michael said. "I don't know how someone with a stamp collection can call anyone a nerd."

"You know about that? Please don't tell Alice," Ralph said worriedly.

"She thinks you're great, I don't think it matters."

"You think so? Because my entire reputation is built on being cool and all." Ralph was still visibly concerned.

"You play badminton with your old teacher because that's the only way she would pass you," Michael laughed. "I'm not sure you can call that cool exactly."

"True," Ralph said. "But it helped me meet her sister, didn't it?" he chuckled. "You know what, Michael?"

"What, Ralph?"

"You're not half bad, we should do this more often."

Michael beamed.

"Maybe I need a little more 'nerd' in my life you know? And anyway, it's safe to say you could be a little cooler," Ralph laughed.

"You're probably right," Michael said, hanging his head, pretending to be sad.

Ralph looked at him, worried he'd make him cry. Michael couldn't help but laugh. Relieved, Ralph smiled. "No, Michael. I KNOW I'm right." (Yeah you are)

After stopping by and picking up some costumes, they set off for Animal Control.

"Are you sure this is the way, Ralph? I mean, I trust you and all, but I think we passed the sign for animal control like 30 minutes ago."

Ralph shook his head. "Michael! If you knew we passed it, why didn't you tell me?"

"I don't know, I just figured you knew."

"Well, I didn't!"

"Sorry!" *You'd think he would pay better attention. I can't do everything around here! I'm not one of those toasters that can umm...do everything.*

"You always do that! Like when we go to the store to buy Mom something for Christmas and you don't tell me she already has it until we get to the car. I just don't get it!"

"I don't know," Michael said.

"It's cool," Ralph said, sighing. "It's just this stupid GPS on my phone never works."

"You'd think something that big could drive FOR you," Michael laughed. "Then we would already be there."

Ralph glared at him.

"But um....I've got a compass if you want to use that?" Michael added, quickly. He rummaged around his fanny pack and pulled it out.

"A compass? Who the devil carries a compass?"

"Doc gave it to me. Look. It points toward those in need! Look!"

Michael handed it to Ralph and sure enough it was pointing back in the direction they came from. Ralph sighed again and turned around.

"You better be right about this. I can only follow freaky compasses so long. It's the principle of the matter, really..."

"Don't worry," Michael said. "I'll let you know when we pass it...this time."

"Thanks."

Animal Control wasn't anything like they'd expected! Located on the bad side of town, they had to take a series of back roads deep into the forest to get there. The front gate was ajar when they arrived. Cue the spooky music....

"This is creepy," Michael said uneasily.

A dim light cast an eerie glow over the vacant parking lot, telling them that they were alone at the compound. Or so they thought?

"Wow, you'd think they would have some security around here or something," Michael said, confused.

"Yeah, or something," Ralph said scanning the area. "Isn't this for the whole county? They must have thousands of animals here!"

"I guess the animals are trustworthy?"

They quietly shut the doors to Ralph's sports car, just in case, and crept toward the front door. Not that they could have kept their entrance much of a secret anyway with what they were wearing. Moe's parents had given Michael an incredibly elaborate spaceman outfit worn by Moe at his fourth birthday. As it was, it was still almost too large for Michael to wear and that was saying something because he isn't a small kid.

The thing is, Moe was a BIG kid. But Michael didn't care, he loved it! The helmet engulfed his head making it hard to see and the matching shoes (which he insisted on wearing) were about three sizes too big. It was awesome. He decided he was definitely 'space-ready.' His fanny pack even fit on the inside!

"I look so good in this outfit, it's almost a shame no one will see it," he told the others.

"Speak for yourself! I can't wait to get out of this. I look ridiculous!" Grohill said.

Michael laughed. "But pet costumes only come in so many styles, you know. And I thought you would prefer the pumpkin one over the princess."

"That's true, it could be worse," Grohill said, examining himself in one of the hubcaps.

"Not for me," Ralph groaned. "I don't know why we're wearing costumes anyway. I can't believe this."

"Ralph, everybody knows you have to disguise yourself when you sneak into somewhere," Michael said matter-of-factly. "Plus, it's MY adventure."

He had taken to using arrogance to cover up his apprehension. On the inside, he was scared out of his mind to break into Animal Control. On the outside, he was as confident and cocky as Lord Piper himself.

Ralph sighed. Since Halloween was only a month away, Moe's parents had insisted on giving them costumes they didn't think would sell. For Michael, that meant a really cool hand-me-down, but for Ralph, well...it was a hand-me-down too, but it wasn't exactly his style.

That is unless Ralph and Moe's younger sister, Tina, shared fashion tips. Michael found this highly unlikely though since they were no longer on speaking terms after breaking up last year. Still, he had to admit that if any guy could make a pink satin ball gown good look it was Ralph.

"Let's just get this over with, nerd. If Mom and Dad figure out I'm out past curfew by four hours, they'll kill me," Ralph said. "And that's without even mentioning you."

"And that's without seeing you in that costume," Michael laughed. "Then they might have some questions."

"Whatever."

Michael frowned. Evidently, the magical brotherly moment they had been having in the car was over. *At least Grohill and I still have a bond. Even though he looks like a pumpkin.* Michael's stomach grumbled. *Mmm... pie.*

Even though the gate had been open, they found the front door locked. *Aha! So they DO have security*, Michael thought. They had better luck with the back, but that was probably because someone had already opened it. They found a rusty old pick-up truck idling by the door.

"Master Michael?" It looks like someone's here, should we turn back?" Grohill asked, his voice trembling.

"Don't be stupid, Grohill," Ralph answered. "We expected someone to be here."

"That's why we have these costumes!" Michael said, overjoyed at his cleverness. "Besides, I only see one car so it's probably only one guy. We can use it for our getaway."

"I HAVE a car, Michael," Ralph said.

Oh yeah...

But as it turns out, it was one BIG car with another car behind it. Bummer.

Michael cracked the door open and crawled inside on his hands and feet to avoid making a lot of noise. Grohill did the same, looking back and forth down the hall apprehensively. Ralph shrugged and walked in.

"What? I don't want to, you know, get Tina's dress dirty," he said blushing. "So where do you think your friend Doc is?"

"I'm not sure," Michael said. "But he might be on this hall labeled 'rabbits.'"

A sheet of paper was taped on the sign in front of them. It was written in crayon and had an arrow toward the 'rabbits' hall. Evidently it was professional enough looking because no one in the group questioned it.

"This place is pretty organized, I'm actually impressed," Ralph said with a look of admiration on his face. "Glad to know my taxes are being put to use."

"Ralph, you don't have a job," Michael said.

"Whatever. Now quick, let's do this and get out of here. I know Doc is important in your quest to defeat Lord Viper or whatever his name is. I need to get home."

"Lord Piper!" Grohill squealed. "Don't mention his name, I get all antsy."

"Whatever. Don't use the word 'antsy,' it's weird."

Grohill looked hurt.

"What I meant was, we need to be fast so we don't get caught," Ralph sighed.

"Get caught!" Grohill shrieked. Suddenly, they heard a noise from down the hall. Moving quickly, they darted into the first room they found and shut the door.

"Yeah, like the shut door won't be enough to give us away," Ralph said.

"Shhh..." Michael said. "Look!"

They'd found the 'rabbits' room. It was something out of a nightmare, or maybe even Principal Goodburn's office. (That could very well easily be the same thing). Rows upon rows of cages lined the walls of a room so large Michael couldn't see the back of it. A light hung from the ceiling, dimly illuminating a half inch of water covering the floor from where the drain system had failed. A table in the far corner was covered in knives of all shapes and sizes. Many of them were stained from recent use.

Grohill dove behind Michael as Michael tried to figure out how to do the same thing himself. *It's just not possible*, he thought. Grohill muttered something, but it was muffled by Michael's leg.

"What did he say?" Ralph asked.

"I said, what is this place?" Grohill asked before hiding himself again.

"It's a tomb," a voice answered.

They turned around and saw Doc shackled to the wall in one of the smaller cages. He didn't look like he'd eaten in weeks, although he'd only been captured that day. His fur was wet and matted, and falling out all over.

He looked old. REALLY old.

"Doc!" Grohill squeaked. "What do you mean?"

"I never thought I would say this, but boy am I glad to see you, Grohill," Doc laughed feebly, each movement causing him visible pain. "And you too, Michael, although it's always a pleasure." Michael smiled weakly. "And who might this er...young man be?" Doc asked, a hint of uncertainty in his voice at the sight of Ralph's costume.

"I'm Michael's brother," Ralph said, kneeling down in front of the cage, his voice soft and reassuring. "And we're here to help you."

"I'm afraid you're too late," the rabbit sighed. "This is where animals come to die!"

"But you're in great shape!" Michael said interrupting him. "At least....you were."

"Oh, I've been sick for some time now, Grohill can attest to that," Doc said sadly. The porcupine nodded. "Sure, I'd gotten good at hiding it, but not to those closest to me. I'd been getting worse, especially in the last week. And you can guess that with the attack, well...." he paused, grimacing. "I'm afraid my body just wasn't up for this..."

"Well, that doesn't matter now, we're going to save you!" Michael said.

"I appreciate it, son, more than you'll ever know. But it doesn't matter now. I'm not sure I'll make it through the night."

"But you can't talk like that!" Ralph said worriedly. "We came here to rescue you!"

"Yeah, you can't give up!" Michael cried.

"You see those knives on the table over the there?" Doc said sadly. "It's my turn next."

"But Doc...what...what do they do with them? Chop carrots?" Grohill asked fearfully.

"I'm not sure. They drugged me so I've been in a half-conscious state all day. When I wake up, the animals are gone. Anyway, you'll never get me out of these chains."

They sat in silence. Their whole rescue was a failure. The costumes, Michael's escape, everything. Lord Piper had won.

"I won't let them hurt you," Michael said, slamming his hand onto the table and knocking the knives to the floor. "Oops." One of them had narrowly missed Grohill's nose, cutting the stem off his pumpkin costume.

"I wouldn't be so sure of that," Chet said, sliding out from beneath the shadows.

What?!?!?! Whoa!!!! Why is HE here?!?

"Who IS that?" Ralph asked. "And why can all of these animals talk? I thought it was just the porcupine and the rabbit?"

Chet laughed. "Your friend there is funny, Mary. He should write a book."

Why does everyone want everyone to write books? No one in their right mind would EVER think of doing that.

"Back off, Chet, before you get yourself hurt!" Grohill said, picking up one of the knives.

This made Chet laugh even harder. "You break in HERE and all you brought was a comedian and a talking pumpkin? Malachi, I thought you were better than that!"

"Where are we?" Michael asked.

"You don't know?" Chet said. "Hasn't he told you?"

Doc shook his head.

"Ha! This is even better than I thought! Martha, this isn't an ordinary Animal Control facility. Well, it WAS until Lord Piper took it over. But he needs animals to do his bidding and what better place to find them than here? The desperate. The abused. After what most of them have been through, Lord Piper seems like loving a father figure! They'll do anything for him! Well, almost all of them."

Chet glared at Doc accusingly. "Lord Piper bought off an employee. Some fool named Jerry Mudwater."

Jerry? Michael thought. *The plot thickens....*

"Oh, but Doc! I don't see why you wouldn't want to follow Lord Piper. After all, he's so gracious. So many of your townspeople have already done so haven't they, Grohill?"

"I don't know what you're talking about."

"Fine...fine...Lie all you want, it won't ruffle my feathers."

"You don't have feathers!" Michael said angrily. "And besides, I thought Dapply made you mad. I thought you wanted to get revenge?" *Not that I believed your story to begin with.*

"Oh, you bought that, did you?"

No!

"Oh my, you are slow," Chet laughed. "I would never turn my back on Dapply. After he's been so kind. So helpful. Haven't you, Dapply?"

To Michael's horror, Dapply, Old Man Goddard and Jerry Mudwater stepped out of the shadows. *They must be big shadows to have hidden so many people...But wait. They're all working together?!?*

"I'm sure you're surprised to see me, Michael," Dapply said, leaning on a tall umbrella.

"Actually, I'm more surprised to see Jerry and Mr. Goddard!"

Dapply ignored him. "After all, how could I have survived that horrible crash outside of Hungry Woody's? But I planned this all along! Yes, a backup plan in case you escaped. I thought you might get away. After all, you are the 'Chosen One,'" he said with a note of venom in his voice. "So that's why I got Jerry here to watch you after Goddard led you into my grasp. As an Animal Control officer. As a waiter....as a search party," he added smiling.

It all makes a lot more sense now.

"You know, to stalk you more or less," Dapply laughed. "I knew you'd try to come here. This plan would NOT fail. You HAD to rescue your pitiful rabbit friend."

"Doc's stronger than you'll ever be!" Michael yelled. Unmoved, Dapply smiled.

"Is he, Michael? Is he? Because the Doc I see is moments from death!"

"What did you do to him?" Ralph said.

"Isn't it obvious?" Dapply smirked eyeing Ralph's attire. "Nothing! He's old, broken....uncooperative."

"I'll never serve Lord Piper," Doc coughed, blood spattering the ground in front of him. "And soon, no other animal will either. Michael's here. You can't stop him."

"And what makes you think an eleven year old can foil years of hard work by many? That's kind of a crazy thing to say, rabbit, I hope you know that."

"Because history's already been written. It's in the prophecy. The good guys win. Not you. Not Lord Piper. We do. For the good of the forest. And Michael here will save us all."

"Then if Michael is such a hero," Dapply said softly. "Let him save you now. Go ahead, I won't interfere." He tossed Michael a key.

They rushed to Doc's side, unchaining him from the wall. Grohill took off his costume (he's naked!) and made it into a pillow to support the rabbit's head. Ralph scanned the room looking for food.

"It's no use now, he's quite right," Doc said sadly. "But don't you let them win, Michael Pumpernickel, you hear me? Don't you let them win!"

307

"But Doc," Michael cried. "I don't know where Lord Piper is. I don't even know where to start!" He felt hopeless as he looked down at the old rabbit.

"The book, Michael, the book!" Doc said. "Do you have it?"

Michael shook his head.

"No matter."

Dapply looked on curiously. Old Man Goddard glanced at Chet. Dapply hadn't told him about that.

"Remember what it said? About the king?"

"Well sure, I don't forget anything I read."

"Good boy," Doc whispered. "I sat here all day and I finally remembered what I'd been told. It isn't a riddle."

"What?" Michael asked. Dapply leaned in closer, clutching something in his suit pocket tightly.

"It isn't a riddle at all!" he laughed. "The stories say that when you receive the book, the town leader is supposed to tell you to go to your grandpa's house. He'll have the answers."

"Who?" Michael said. "The town leader?"

"No, your grandpa."

"Write that down, write that down!" Dapply said quickly, handing Jerry Mudwater a pad of paper. Jerry eyed Dapply nervously and frantically began drawing a picture of his own grandpa. Jerry couldn't write.

"It's so hard to get good help these days, " Dapply sighed, smoothing the wrinkles in his suit coat. Chet gritted his teeth, but kept his eyes trained on Michael. "Now," Dapply continued. "Goddard, if you could hold on to this book for me and go stand guard outside, I think it's time we taught these boys a lesson. Isn't that right, Chet?"

"Whoa, wait a second!" Michael said, catching Dapply off-guard.

The villain paused, fidgeting with his umbrella. "What do you want? Can't you see I'm about to kill your friend?"

"Well yeah..." Michael said, stalling. He was hoping to come up with a really good plan of escape, he just needed some time. Goddard glared at him and left the room. Michael looked down at his favorite shirt for courage. "It's just that. What IS Lord Piper up to anyway? Why does he need all of these animals?"

"Why, Michael! I'm so glad you asked!" Dapply said smiling. "I thought you'd never ask." He looked elated.

It's working! Michael thought excitedly. Except he kind of wanted to know what Dapply was going to say because he wouldn't have a lot of time to come up with a plan while listening.

"He has an evil plan, Michael. An evil, evil plan. And I...CAN'T tell you what it is!" Dapply laughed. Chet and Jerry Mudwater joined in uncomfortably.

That didn't help.

"Um.....so like, can I ask more questions?" Michael said disappointedly. His plan was NOT working.

"No, Michael. I don't think so."

Hoping for the element of surprise, Dapply attacked first, drawing a small dagger from inside his umbrella. He lunged, barely missing Michael as he dove to protect Doc. The key in hand, Michael struck Dapply across the face, stunning him. Michael grabbed the rabbit to retreat to the far side of the room. Unfortunately, he tripped on the oversized shoes of the spaceman costume and came crashing down right in front of Chet. Not that the shoes really had anything to do with it. He always trips.

The otter smiled wickedly as he moved in for the kill. Unfortunately for him, and not really anyone else, he was downed by Grohill, a crazy look in the porcupine's eyes. Quickly hiding Doc in one of the cabinets, Michael rushed to help Ralph, who was locked in a furious standoff with Dapply.

Fearful for his life, Jerry Mudwater bolted for the door, but found it locked. He looked around frantically for an escape, but found none. He dropped to the floor, pleading for his life, but no one listened.

Together, Ralph and Michael overpowered Dapply, forcing him to the ground. Feeling that victory was near they began to cheer until they saw that Grohill's battle with Chet wasn't going very well. The porcupine had a bad cut on the top of his head which was bleeding at an alarming rate.

"Grohill, get out of there!" Ralph yelled, not wanting to lose their advantage over Dapply.

"The only way he's getting out of here is if he's dead," Dapply sneered. "And that goes for ALL of you!"

"It doesn't seem to me that you're in a position to say things like that," Michael said confidently.

"I admit, you've got me cornered," Dapply said hanging his head. He winked at Chet. "But what are you going to do now? Kill me?" He locked eyes with Michael.

"Umm...well...ummm." Michael didn't think Crispin would like him anymore if he killed someone.

"Of course not," Ralph yelled reassuring his brother. "We're going to call the cops and you're going to be arrested!"

"Wearing that?" Dapply laughed.

Ralph considered it for a moment. An awkward silence hung over the room.

"Ralph!"

"Fine, fine..." Dapply continued. "Call the cops, see if they get here in time. After all, I'm not afraid to kill. See?" He turned to Jerry Mudwater, driving the blade into his chest. Jerry shrieked and collapsed to the ground.

"And the world has one....less...coward," Dapply said slowly for emphasis, wiping the blood off of his blade. "His purpose was served. Now, Michael. Do you really want to resist me now that you've seen what I can do? Let me tell you, that wouldn't be...how do I say it? Wise."

"You're the worst organist EVER!" Michael said angrily, still shocked at Jerry's death.

"What do musical talents have to do with anything right now?" Dapply asked, thrown off.

"Nothing, I'm just mad at you!" Michael said.

"Yeah!" Ralph added.

(Yeah! Just go with it...)

"Nah," Chet said.

Suddenly, Jerry wasn't dead! He grabbed Dapply's dagger and sliced him across the back. The organist yelled in pain, blood quickly staining his jacket.

"This was an import!" he screamed.

Surprised, Chet let go of Grohill long enough for the porcupine to limp behind Michael and Ralph.

"How do I say this, Dapply?" Michael asked. "The tables...have...turned."

"You won't get away with this," Dapply said staggering to the door. "Not for long. I'll hunt down you for the rest of your life. Those you love will pay. You'll pay for my jacket. And in the end? Lord Piper will win!"

And with that, Dapply and Chet fled the room. They heard a commotion outside and the sound of sirens drowned out by Dapply's angry yells. Ralph turned to Michael and winked.

"You called the cops?!?" Michael asked, surprised.

"Sure. I gave them the heads up that there were dangerous criminals here who were using the facility to further their own evil plans."

"That's...that's...."

"Brilliant!" Grohill said.

"I'll say," Michael said, smiling. "I guess we should go thank them."

"Right..." Ralph said uneasily. "Yeah, I didn't really mention anything about talking animals, or an evil fox. I think it's probably best if we just, you know, go."

"Isn't that obstructing justice?" Michael asked. "Or like, fleeing the scene of a crime?"

"I don't know. I think we have a few minutes. It sounds like they have their hands full with Goddard, Dapply and Chet," Ralph laughed. They could still hear the organist struggling outside.

"Thank goodness."

Relieved, Ralph and Michael embraced in exhaustion.

"But no seriously, I'm glad that's over," Ralph said, pulling away quickly.

Michael laughed, not sure if Ralph was talking about the fight or their hug.

"I just want to take off this stupid dress."

"I don't know, Ralph," Michael laughed. "I'm starting to get used to it. The color looks good with your skin color."

Ralph glared at him. "Just because I helped you defeat that guy from the band doesn't mean we're friends now or anything."

Amazing. "Grohill, we're still friends, right?

"Yeah maybe," the porcupine said. The cut on the top of his head had stopped bleeding. "But you're going to have to promise me you won't let me get picked up by Animal Control. This place is sketchy."

"I kind of take offense at that," Jerry said, clutching his chest. The others had forgotten he was there. "Although I don't think I work for them anymore."

They all laughed.

"Jerry," Michael said. "What did Dapply mean by evil plan? Is it bad?"

Jerry chuckled. "Is evil EVER good?"

"Well, no," Michael said confused. "I just can't figure out what he's up to."

"Most of the details are a little above my pay grade, mind you," Jerry said. "But I know he and the villagers have some history. Bad history. He wants to ruin their lives by destroying their homes. But he's got bigger plans than that if you ask me. That's why he's going to sell those trendy necklaces out here. You know, to people and stuff."

Trendy necklaces? Does he mean the jewelry he mentioned on the talk show? Why do I feel like I should know more about that....

"Hey, where's Doc?" Grohill asked.

Aha! Doc! I knew I'd forgotten someone. Now where did I put him? Michael wondered.

When they found the rabbit, his eyes were closed. Grohill squeaked and embraced him. "Hey there, Doc," he said weakly. "How are you feeling?"

When the rabbit was unresponsive he continued. "You'll be better soon. We'll all be better." Tears were streaming down his face, mixing with blood.

"I didn't get to tell him I'm sorry," Grohill said.

"I didn't get to tell him goodbye," Michael cried.

"I just met that guy, what's his name again?" Ralph asked. Michael glared at him. "What?" he said. Sighing, Ralph picked up Doc's body and began to walk out of the room. "Let's give him a proper burial."

"He's not dead yet!"

"Yes he is!" Ralph said, a tear forming in his eye. He turned away hoping no one had seen him. He was surprised at his own emotions. For someone who hadn't cried during that really sad movie I can't remember the name of, he was oddly choked up. "He's dead, guys."

They knew he was right.

"Umm...pardon me," Jerry said. "But I'm still here and I'm NOT dead yet." He was pale in the face.

"You look you need medical attention," Michael said.

"Yeah, well...that's kind of what I was getting at." Jerry collapsed onto the ground.

"What should we do with him?" Michael asked.

"What do you mean? Let's leave him!" Grohill said. "He's working for Lord Piper! Look what he did to Doc!" The porcupine glanced sadly at the rabbit in Ralph's arms.

"But he's like...a human!" Michael said.

(Good observation)

"That's why we should leave him!"

"Grohill..."

"How about I carry Jerry and YOU carry Doc, Michael?" Ralph sighed. "We NEED to get out of here!" Dapply's cries had died down and it was likely that the police would want to check the inside of the facility.

"Oh, junk, you're right!"

Ralph transferred the rabbit to Michael and they snuck out the back of the building. When they got back to his car, Ralph called emergency services and left an anonymous tip that there was a man with a deep knife wound in need of their help. They made Jerry comfortable and left.

"Shouldn't we have just taken Jerry to the authorities?"

"Are you kidding me? He'll be fine," Ralph said. "I saw this in the movie, Animal Control." (Ironic)

"You watched that? Mom said you weren't allowed to?"

"Umm....it was Moe's idea."

"But the guy in that movie died!" Michael said sadly.

"You watched it too?"

"Umm...it was Oliver's idea?"

"Whatever. This time it'll be different. Jerry will be fine."

They left.

They buried Doc by the willow trees at the park. Crazy Jack lay nearby, sleeping on one of the benches.

"He'll look after him," Michael said.

"You mean Doc, or Crazy Jack?" Ralph asked. "Crazy Jack is crazy!"

"Yeah...but we couldn't bury him any closer to the river because that could be damaging to the water supply," Grohill said.

"True," Michael sighed. "I can't believe it's over."

It had only been a week, but it had been the craziest week of his life. He'd been chased by an old man, a deranged organist and a guy with like six jobs. AND he'd lived to tell about it. Now they were all in jail. He wouldn't have to worry anymore!

"Don't you still have to like, defeat this Lord Viper guy?" Ralph asked, confused.

"I don't know," Michael said. "Everyone seemed to think that I was some sort of hero in all this, but...I'm just not so sure. I DO think I was able to do some good though and I'm proud of that. But Dapply, Old Man Goddard and Jerry are in jail. What else can Lord Piper do? He doesn't have anyone left! The Twins? Not alone. They don't do anything without Dapply. I think it's only a matter of time before the villagers escape. And well...I don't think they need me for that. I think my time is done."

"But Master Michael...what about Doc? What about what he said? You know, about your grandpa?" Grohill asked.

"Wait...how can you talk?" Michael said. "Animal Control was in the forest, but here? You need the trees!"

"What do you mean?" Ralph said. "They can't always talk? I was going to go home and have a word with Prometheus! I think he took my sweatshirt."

Uh oh...

Grohill smiled, pointing to the newest accessory hanging from his neck. "I swiped it from Chet. He's probably missing it really bad right about now," he laughed.

"Why, you dog," Michael smiled, always wanting to use that phrase.

"I thought he was a porcupine?" Ralph said, confused.

"The necklaces help animals talk," Grohill explained, "because they're made out of the magical trees from the forest."

Ohhhhhhhhh...

"I didn't realize it at first, but it totally makes sense! We've seen one of these before. First, at the village. Then, on Chet. Every time we see them..."

"It's because of Lord Piper!" Michael finished, eyes wide. "The animal on the tree with the sunglasses must be a fox!"

"What?" Ralph asked.

"Nevermind," Michael said excitedly. "If Lord Piper is making these necklaces from the trees, he's destroying the forest! Does he mean to cut down the whole thing?"

"I don't know, Master Michael, but we have bigger problems. If he takes away all of the trees, then only the animals wearing these necklaces can talk. And if he can control who gets the necklaces, he can pretty much control who talks. Game over for the good guys."

"But why does he want to sell them to humans like Jerry said?" Michael asked. "Humans can already talk."

"I wish YOU wouldn't," Ralph said sarcastically.

"Because he doesn't want to just control the forest, Michael. He wants to control the world! Look at what it says on the side of the necklace."

Grohill handed Michael the medallion.

"I didn't see this before," he said, shuddering at the memory of the last time he'd held one of these. He turned it over carefully and began reading.

"It is foolish to resist that which is inevitable. It is foolish to resist that which is good." Michael frowned, handing the necklace back to Grohill.

"What the heck does THAT mean?" he wondered. "It's catchy..."

"I don't know, Master Michael. But I have a feeling that Lord Piper truly believes he's doing the right thing. And that scares me more than anything. We don't even know what effect the necklaces have on humans."

"It could be anything..." Michael said in awe. "This is WAY bigger than we thought. But you really think I'm the one who has to stop him? How? Why?"

"I don't know, Master Michael. I don't know."

They sat in stunned silence, processing what they had discovered.

"Then I guess I'm not done yet, am I?" Michael asked, sadly.

"No, Master Michael, I don't think you are."

Less than an hour later they swerved into Grandpa Pumpernickel's driveway, barely missing an elderly couple on their afternoon stroll. Naturally, the couple didn't even notice. Michael breathed a sigh of relief.

"That was close."

"Whatever," Ralph said. "I have to go home because Mom has left me like three million messages on my voicemail. I'll come pick you up tonight, okay?" Michael nodded. "And you know, be safe and stuff."

As Ralph sped out of the driveway, Michael gazed at the house. It was huge. And awesome. *How can grandpa afford this again?* he wondered. Shrugging he walked up to the door and rang the doorbell. *That's the nicest doorbell I've ever heard*, he thought. He sat down on the stoop and waited for someone to come to the door. Grohill paced around in the grass.

"I don't know what we'll find here, Master Michael, but if Doc believed your grandpa can help, I do too. He might have the secret to defeating Lord Piper!"

"I don't know. Grandpa's a cool guy and all. I just don't see him being into this kind of shady stuff. He won't even go to Bingo on Tuesdays because he said you have to cheat to win."

They laughed. When Michael's grandpa answered the door he frowned at them.

"Why aren't you in school, Michael?

"Umm...because I need your help."

Grandpa Pumpernickel sighed. "I knew this day would come," he said sadly. "But this isn't a good time."

"Sure it is, Grandpa," Michael said standing up. "Forget what I said about needing help." He needed to change his tactics. It didn't look like Grandpa Pumpernickel wanted to talk. Oh, but he would MAKE him talk. "You didn't come to my birthday party. Maybe we can celebrate now? After all, I'm extremely hungry. I haven't really eaten all that much recently. Just some Vanilla Squares, juice, jelly, berries...My fanny pack is almost empty."

Grandpa Pumpernickel looked at them nervously. "I'm sorry, Michael, I really am. I had bingo the night of your party. I just couldn't make it. I was in the state finals!"

What?!

"Nevermind. You need to go."

"No, Grandpa. I need to be here."

"Michael, when I say that this isn't a good time, I mean that it isn't a 'good time!'"

There are those quotes again. But Michael wasn't ready to let his grandpa stop them. Doc didn't die in vain! He grabbed the door and pushed it open.

"Michael, no!"

Sitting before them at the kitchen table sat Old Man Goddard, looking very comfortable and very not in jail. And very, very happy.

"Why hello, Michael! Nice of you to drop in."

327

Now I know a lot of you are thinking. "Wow, what a terrible way to end a book. I mean, why give such a cliffhanger when you can just end it?" Well, I, your storyteller and gracious narrator, have good news and bad news. Which would you like first?

Ah, the good news. Somehow I knew you'd pick that! Well, fortunately for me (you didn't think the good news was for you, did you?), there is not only going to be one more book in this series, but two! Yes, two! That means that I have a job for a least a few more years. We'll get to spend more time together. That's not so bad, is it? Well...it shouldn't be.

But don't you want to see what happens to Michael? After all, he's just an ordinary kid like you are. Or once were. Or still are, but shouldn't be? I don't know. The good news is that there is no bad news because a trip to Burlwood Forest is almost always worth it. And if it's not then it should be. Does that make sense? Until next time!

John Choquette is the author of the Burlwood Forest Trilogy and a number of picture books for children of all ages. His work has appeared in numerous online and print publications, and he's a staff member for an emerging music web site and a college athletic blog. He received a B.A. in journalism from The University of North Carolina at Chapel Hill, and lives in the Triangle Area with his awesome wife, Anna.

Follow him on Twitter @burlwoodforest, and at his web site, www.burlwoodforest.com, to stay up-to-date on the amazing things that he's up to.

38227104R00186

Made in the USA
Lexington, KY
28 December 2014